Personal Freedom

Personal Freedom

On Finding Your Way to the Real World

Arthur Deikman, M.D.

Grossman Publishers
A Division of The Viking Press
New York
1976

First published in 1976 by Grossman Publishers
625 Madison Avenue, New York, N.Y. 10022
Published simultaneously in Canada by
The Macmillan Company of Canada Limited
Printed in the United States of America

Library of Congress Cataloging in Publication Data
Deikman, Arthur.
    Personal freedom.

    Includes bibliographical references.
    1. Self-actualization (Psychology)   2. East and West.
3. Deikman, Arthur.   I. Title.
BF637.S4D44   158   76-2053
ISBN 0-670-54825-1

Acknowledgments

Collins-Knowlton-Wing, Idries Shah and Jonathan Cape, Ltd:
From *The Way of the Sufi*, Dutton, 1969; © 1968 by Idries Shah.
From *Thinkers of the East*, Penguin, 1971; © 1971 by Idries Shah.
From *The Magic Monastery*, Dutton, 1972; © 1972 by Idries Shah.
From *The Exploits of Mulla Nasrudin*, Dutton, 1972; © 1966 by Mulla
Nasrudin Enterprises Ltd. No part of the works reprinted herein may be
reproduced without express written permission from the author's agent,
Collins-Knowlton-Wing, New York, N.Y., A. P. Watt & Son, London.

Schocken Books Inc.: From Volume I *Tales of the Hasidim: Early Masters*
by Martin Buber. Copyright © 1947 by Schocken Books Inc. From Volume
II *Tales of the Hasidim: Later Masters* by Martin Buber. Copyright © 1948
by Schocken Books Inc.

Charles E. Tuttle Co., Inc.: "Muddy Road" from *Zen Flesh, Zen Bones* by
Paul Reps.

To my father,
Jules Deikman
1896—1975

In the amplitude of God's earth,
why have you fallen asleep in a prison?
—Rumi

Acknowledgments

Etta, my wife, my life partner, is partner to this book as well. Cathy and Susy, my daughters, gave me the benefit of their fresh and direct response. They and Etta aided me in more ways than I can say.

Many friends helped with this book. Particularly generous with their encouragement and time were Thomas Hanna, George Leonard, John Levy, and Michael Murphy. They often gave me energy when mine had ebbed.

Versions of the manuscript were read and critized by Bob and Carol Barbee, Arthur Colman, Richard Cramer, Elsie Deikman, Silas Hoadley, Don Sandner, Steve Schoen, Alan Skolnikoff, Ronald Spinka, and Frances Smith. They helped prune excesses, exposed laziness, and encouraged clarity.

Dick Grossman, my publisher and editor, sponsored me with a confidence that was aid in itself.

Not least, Helen Landreth typed the book and its many drafts—quickly, enthusiastically, generously.

Contents

Personal Freedom

1.

Who Are the Realists?

Something is wrong. I've noticed it for a long time, as if there is something odd or unreal about the world. Most of the time I'm busy with what I'm doing and don't notice, but, sooner or later, that persistent nagging awareness emerges again, telling me that something is peculiar about my view of things, and everyone else's, too.

I don't mean that the world seems to be collapsing—starvation, atomic bombs, pollution—it isn't just those things, drastic as they may be. There is something still more basically wrong. It's as if you went to the movies and there was something odd about the projector or something strange about the camera that was used to take the movies in the first place. The images themselves seem normal, but the way it is put together is out of sequence, or taken at different speeds, or the perspective keeps changing. That's what I mean. There is something basically wrong with the structure of the world—as we have been taught to see it—but you might not notice it for a long while. It's not until you really examine your experience that you catch sight of the peculiarities. It just isn't the way you've been told. Let me give you an example:

Time makes no sense. It really doesn't apply to me; it doesn't fit. My hair gets thin and I can't stay up all night the way I used to. But *I* don't change. At my center I'm transparent; I'm looking out a window at everything that passes by. Time passes (I observe) and I will die (I am told), but these things don't fit that clear place where I am. Isn't that your experience, too? You get older and everyone around you gets older and you see your birthdays clicking away like numbers on a gasoline pump, but I'll bet there is something inside of you that doesn't feel it is changing at all; inside you're like some kind of mirror, reflecting everything without absorbing it. The mirror doesn't change. You watch time pass, and perhaps believe it when people tell you that you'll die—but it really doesn't fit that clear place inside. Time fits my body and the world I see, but it doesn't fit *me*.

Or consider it from another angle: Time flows like a river, it would seem. Yesterday, today, and tomorrow seem like a road stretching far behind and far ahead. Yet outside my window is an actual road, and on that road any place seems the same as ten feet ahead or ten feet behind—but it's not that way with Time. Ten seconds past and ten seconds ahead is nothingness, just smoke, whereas *Now*, this moment, where I am, is clear and bright. On either side in Time, there's nothing similar to Now, only memories (the past) or imaginings (the future). The place you were ten seconds ago has vanished, and what is the place ten seconds ahead? There is nothing there. It's very odd. Doesn't it strike you, now that you notice, that something is wrong? The "road of Time" is a thought—and the thought doesn't fit.

You have been told that you are fundamentally alone. "We enter the world alone and we exit alone," and so forth. Just you, confronting the universe. And what is the nature of the universe? Our scientific "realists" tell us it is a fascinating, orderly biochemical machine composed of electrical charges, but meaningless, purposeless, and indifferent. So— you are alone in an indifferent world. You are a highly sophisticated "biocomputer" in a highly sophisticated "hyperspace." Congratulations!

But is that your actual experience? Remember those times when you were touched by something impalpable emanating from that "outside" realm of people and things. Music, nature, sports, prayer, sex, insight, drugs, encounter, friendship, or love—a moment when you felt connected, merging, exalted. I'm talking about those special times when you felt a joyous reverence and gratitude and mystery and recognition, at finding yourself, once again, at that place. Of course, you can "explain" it and nothing need change. The mechanical puppet cosmos can clank along forever: just tell yourself that those experiences, "mystical" or otherwise, are the infantile derivatives of wishes, fears, and early memories. It's simple. But is that what they feel like? Talk to children and see if they experience such things. Consider carefully whether those special moments really fit the vapid formula: "Infantile derivatives." Isn't that explanation something you have swallowed,

3

force-fed, like an infant, indeed, but have never been able to digest? It's indigestible because it doesn't fit, that's why. It's another swindle, like Time.

You are told you are basically alone—in empty space. Yet, when you love, are you alone? When you look, unguarded, into another's eyes, clear place to clear place, are you alone? When you wholeheartedly engage in work or play, are you alone? There is only one way to be alone: by *thinking* about it. The thought creates the aloneness; the concept is the problem. "Aloneness" does not fit experience.

When mathematics and chemistry define your world, it has no meaning; the world dries up. But, for *you,* as you walk the streets, engage others, live your life, your world is charged with meaning, filled with purposes, conflicted or aligned, at every level. Do the words "random" and "meaningless" really fit what you *feel,* what you experience, moment by moment—or are they something you have been told, something you now *think*?

Let's go a step further: Who or what are you?

If I ask myself that question and take a look to see, it's very curious indeed. I thought that *I* was happy, that *I* was thinking, that *I* was seeing, but when I pause and look inside it seems as if I've been looking out a window at "my" feelings, at "my" sensations, and at "my" thoughts—such as this one. If I'm looking at them, how can they be *me*? There is some kind of awareness, something basic that observes everything, and, although I usually don't notice because it is drowned out by all the noise, it's always there. If I turn back to find myself, look inward to the deepest, the very heart of me where I actually live, that awareness is me. It seems to have been there always, just as it is, while everything else changes. Try an experiment, right now. Close your eyes and ask yourself if you have disappeared. What's your answer? Now, cover your ears so sounds are absent—have you disappeared? No matter what part of the world or your thoughts or your feelings you make go away, *you* stay there. Now, what is that you? That's what I'm talking about—that place. And, in fact, it's not even a place, it's you. That's what you are and that's what I am. Until I ask that question, I'm a psychiatrist, a male, a husband, Arthur Deikman. But when I ask that question and look to see, I'm that window, that lookout, that awareness. It isn't just a theory; it's what my experience actually is and yours, too. It's really very obvious, but you were told nothing about it through all your years of school. The most basic factor of your existence, the one thing you experience indisputably, your own aware self, is never mentioned. Everything else is: the everything else that is not you.

Let's look at the wisdom you've been taught, your guidebook to the human condition:

Sample 1: Satisfaction doesn't last. We're used to that principle and accept it, but isn't that a strange arrangement? You work for a goal that evaporates when it's in your hand. "True, so true, that's the way life is. . . ." What an odd life!

Sample 2: Nothing's perfect—particularly you. Everything's flawed, everything's a little off. How come? It's not so obvious that life must be defective. Would you have constructed it that way? No. So why would God? It doesn't make sense.

You see, you've been taught that that's the way everything is. You're even annoyed that I bother you about it. But stop, consider what you've been taught: time, aloneness, dissatisfaction, imperfection, identity; are they really logical? Are they facts? Are they "realistic" or have you been swindled, conned so well that it feels like home to you? It's almost funny! You thought you were being mature, adult, strong, looking life straight in the eye, hardly flinching. Maybe you've been duped. Maybe you've been living in a crazy house all this time.

Let's look around. (Perhaps there's a door.) Let's be curious and ask, "How did I learn about reality? Who are the realists?"

2.

Learning About Reality

In the Womb

We begin as awareness floating in our mother's ocean. We are warm and at ease, but do not "know" it. Slowly, we grow and move and sensations flower: pressure, vibrations, motion. In the beginning, there are no needs, no wants. Food comes to us continuously, permeating the blood. There is no need to breathe; oxygen, like food, flows effortlessly through us and our world. The temperature is even and the fetus is supported by the womb. There is neither satisfaction nor dissatisfaction. Movement occurs, vibrations are transmitted, and chemicals may change, but, by and large, the womb world is a constant one with little stress with which we must contend. We are called a fetus at that stage but we are really a part of our mother's body, not more separate than her own heart, held back from merging completely with her only by the placental membrane through which we "breathe" and "eat."

Not at birth does awareness begin, but months before. While still in our mother's womb we become aware. Consider:

Infants may be born prematurely, one or two months early, and yet they function psychologically, even though, by the calendar, they have not yet been born. The capacity for awareness does not depend on emerging from the womb nine months after conception. Inside the womb, the fetus senses the world and can respond. For example, a loud noise will cause a fetus to stir. If you tap on the mother's abdomen at the same time, the tap and the noise will become linked; the fetus will then move in response to a tap; it has "remembered." Microscopic studies show its nervous system is not fully developed, but a nervous system *is* there, responsive to a degree we cannot determine, as we have no idea of what systems of perception and response may exist without neurons, or with use of neurons we call "immature." Premature infants are responsive, and we must conclude that the human organism before its birth is very much alive, in mind as well as body.

"Well," you say, "we may be aware and capable of 'learning' in our mother's body, but who can really remember what we learned?"

There are many kinds of memory. For example, our bodies remember. Our posture, shaped by tension, our rigid jaws and tight bellies—the "armoring" of Reich—encode the pain and fear of early years. Release the tension, soften the armor, and the past floods forth in emotion, images, a word, a gesture. Yet, what our bodies had remembered every day of our lives, our minds had not recalled.

The very pattern of our life remembers. We may choose our "luck," the style of our mates, the form of our work, our personal myth, in order to repeat, to remember the past. We react in old patterns—the "transference" of Freud—remembering by emotions. With these strategies, we repeat without awareness the pain and fear of early years, controlling and preserving them at the same time. How early are those memories? Very early, before words, sometimes; so early that a tingling in the lips may be all we can recover. The memory is there, but it guides our life without our knowing.

If you agree we are aware within the womb, "listening" to life, "remembering," you may still ask, "How can we be taught; what is the route whereby we learn?"

Our mother's speech, her laughter, her crying, her anger are vibrations transmitted through her body as well as through the air; they pervade the womb as well as the outer world. Vibrations speak in their own way: the fetus knows no words, but it can feel. In India, sounds are used to transform man. Mantras—syllables and words—repeated endlessly, are said to reach each cell, stilling the mind and setting free the energy of bliss. Mystic masters, scientists in their own right, claim each sound has its own vibration energy, producing its own effect, to be prescribed according to the need and possibility of each human being.

In daily life we can sense the meaning of a muffled conversation. Anger, joy, and sadness sing their own songs, without need for words. We feel them—why not also within the womb? An experiment: Subjects are asked to imagine emotions, then press a delicate button that records the subtle pattern their pressure makes, forward and back, strong or soft, wavering, increasing or declining. The different subjects give the same pattern for each emotion; we touch in the same way. Deep in our being is a code of feeling, of touch, vibration—a language in our cells.

Our mother spoke to us in many ways, months before we left her: the rich vibrations of her voice conveyed her feelings; her hormones signaled stress; her muscles tensed and changed the pressure of our world. Were there yet other languages and channels for our pre-born mind? Pure energy may be a route for knowing. Acupuncturists say an energy permeates and flows throughout our bodies, affected by pressure and by heat at key points along "meridians." Kirlian photography shows pulsing zones of "bioplasma" surrounding living forms, responsive to emotion. Electrical currents on the skin change with emotion and can be measured to indicate the meaning charge of words. Salamanders grow back limbs, guided by the change in their limbs' electric field. And if ESP is real, what barrier can exist between a mother and her unborn child?

We were bathed in energy within our mothers, pulsations rocked us in our sleep. Hormone messages came by blood and sounds vibrated in our cells. Information perfused our first world.

What did we learn? Much more than we believe. The serenity, agitation, or depression of a mother goes quickly to the womb by all the messengers of body and mind. Subtleties of voice and movement paint a portrait of the world. Some persons shine with an aura of joy; calmness and easiness streams from them like light. We feel good in their presence. They say, without words, "The world is okay"; "No cause for fear"; "I'm with you"; "I like you"; "We're one." From another person comes alarm; posture, voice and odor warn of pain, of danger stalking the world. Distrust speaks: "Stay away"; "I'm afraid"; "I dislike you"; "Bitterness is life." Basic messages, day by day; cosmologies of feeling transmitted through a chain of generations.

As we flowered in our mother's womb, we were learning, listening to the messages that told us of the world, how it is, what we could expect, how we should approach our swelling life.

And then we were born.

The Pelvic Journey

Although we think of emergence into the world as the first great shock, it must have been tremendous relief after the inconceivable stress of the pelvic journey. When birth begins, the world of the womb is utterly transformed from placidity and ease to utter violence and chaotic tension. The contrast with the previous state is so great that it will probably not be matched during the entire period of life that follows. The uterine muscle contracts with enormous power, and the pressure upon the fetus multiplies many times. Its body is jammed and twisted into the pelvic tunnel with such force that the head may be molded to accommodate the passage. The mother herself is in a state of maximum stress, mobilizing all her reserves in order to cope. Within the womb, the world has gone mad, convulsing and churning. A contraction ceases, and there is a period of quiet and rest—and then it occurs again and again and again and again. Each time the forces and pressures are stronger and the fetal functioning more compromised. The once free-floating world becomes totally constricted until all freedom is gone; the arms are pinned to the sides and the head is twisted, stretched, and bent in its journey through the pelvic outlet. During that passage, the umbilical cord providing oxygen and food may become compressed and occluded, or the cord may be wrapped around the neck and shut off or decrease the oxygen needed by the brain. Thus, suffocation may be added to the onslaught. The turmoil reaches a zenith and then resolves with great suddenness as the head pops free; the body follows soon after. Initiation of breathing and the security of the mother's arms mark the beginning of the next phase.

Is that really how it feels? Perhaps I've given an adult's view of something that is only a physical process, with no mind or memory to take notes. We don't remember being born, so how can we tell?

True, we think we don't remember, yet there may be memories deeply buried in us. They may be memories of a different kind—not in terms of vision, but in a physical form, in sensory patterns different from those forms that develop later in maturity. When patients were given LSD, week after week, for months, they showed a similar pattern of experience. It seemed that each person re-experienced his birth. Mentally and physically he portrayed the pelvic journey with all the features that go with it: suffocation, pain, strain, and rest. Trapped, compressed, in endless chaos, the journey ended in explosive, expansive bliss, in utter quiet and flooding light. These "memories" were so explicit, so correct in detail, they suggest our birth creates a pattern around which we group events of later life. Birth may be a way of classifying life. If that is so, what could we learn from being born? Such an overwhelming journey might begin a "need" to escape and to expand, a need for power, to control, and a fear of helplessness. Linked with these needs and fears may be the "memory" of serenity, of paradise, of a state without confusion, pain, or struggle. From the moment of our birth we may begin a journey toward a goal whose initial form lies behind us, but whose path will carry us to something we have never felt before nor seen.

3.

Lessons Outside the Womb

Automatization

Now begins a process that is both the magic means and the relentless curse of our lives: automatization. Whatever we do becomes a pattern—automatic—no longer needing our attention. Watch an infant struggle to its feet, intensely focused on its basic task; it sways perilously, staggers forward, sways again, and falls back solidly on its rump. Totally absorbed, it tries again—and falls again. Yet, two months later, it stands without concern and toddles rapidly to its mother, all attention fixed on the bottle in her hand. An adult, learning to drive, sweats to make the clutch and shift work together, looking up desperately to steer and looking down to do the gears. A year later, he or she drives down the freeway, sixty miles an hour, chatting with a friend about a party the night before. We learn to move and grasp and drive a car and a thousand other skills and, having learned, run off with our attention fixed on something else.

We learn everything. We must even learn to see. The first world of mixed-up colors, changing shapes, and shifting brightness required our attention, too. When adults, blind since birth, have sight restored, they do not see a world suddenly found. Light and color in pure confusion assault their minds. Weeks of effort finally yield success: a pencil can be recognized, held up and down. But shift the pencil to the horizontal and it is lost again. Another lesson must be learned. So much work is needed that adults with new-found sight sometimes refuse the gift, retreating to the world of sound and touch already fashioned since their early years.

Our bodies teach us, too. The mouth informs our mind with openings and closings. A man holds out a box, lid closed. "Open the box, baby!" It's a problem for the baby's mind, and he turns the box, puzzled. Finally, he opens wide his mouth, *then* he opens the lid. His body functions lead his mind, providing patterns for his thought. Those pattern modes respond to need—and to reward, reward determined by his culture's need. Many forces teach us how to live.

Learning, learning, every minute, every day, learning about reality from those who learned from those who learned, back through the generations. Learning patterns, layer on layer, building up our world. From one pattern to the next we move, each lesson filed away, programmed now to function automatically without awareness of the process steps. We are automatized, our attention freed for other things. Freedom, yes, but slavery, too, for a curse is latent in the power: the first encounter cannot be regained. What was it like to stagger to our feet and, lurching, take our first steps across an enormous room? What was it like, that first movie, concert, beach? We pay a price: the freshness and the richness of our "beginner's mind."

We learned to hear, to see, to think in a world of objects, and we could not learn about the object world without selection. We are taught to be selective, to pay close notice to the shape of things. A mother holds a ball and says a word; baby repeats the sound, reaching for the bright, round color, "Ball, ball!" Day after day, the baby learns. The ball, the mother, and the world are jealous beings. They demand subordination of all competing things: the background must subside so they can stand forth, commanding recognition. Objects and their meanings rule our day; as we grow older, form, shape, and boundaries crowd out the sensual. Color and texture recede from sight; no longer chosen first, they fade in intensity. Thus, the world changes as we learn, according to our lessons.

Selection has a price, and we forget what we left behind. Our infant years are blank, and early childhood, too. We seem to have emerged at five or six into a world already there, not remembering our creative role, not recalling how it was before our school began, not knowing that we learned it all.

The Development of the Sense of Self

Imagine the infant's world: Shifting fields of sensations within shifting levels of sleep and waking. Swirling mists of warm sleep giving way to bright color and simple patterns, mixed with gnawing feelings, persistent and demanding; then muscle tensings and crying sounds; then warmth and pleasure and the smell of mother, liquid warmth and mouth tensions; then dissolving into darkness; and then the light and color, discomforts—beginning patterns—on and on. Memoryless, the flow holds all attention. Gradually, the patterns form: mother's smell and comforting pressure, activity of eyes and mouth, hands grasping, mother's sounds.

Sensations separate the baby from the world, those that go and those that stay, becoming "inside" and "outside" much later on. Now they just come and go; pain, hunger, touch, and smell are the teachers. Pain draws a line around the edge of fingers, and vision tidies up the clutter of light. Together they teach the body as the baby's will begins to command. Grab the bottle; grab the nose; pat the face that smiles. Crawl to the warmth; pull back from the fire; grab the food; stuff the mouth; drop the glass; move the fingers for the eyes to see. Pain, loss, and intention separate the world into us and them. Mother leaves, but pain remains; the arm can be moved, but the crib stays still. Yet the separation of "inner" from "outer" is really not so clear. Crying can summon others and thus affect the inner pain; the baby may not be able to move from the holding arms. What is cause and what effect comes later. For the moment, patterns rule the day and may continue, if the culture wills, without an automatic road of Time. At first, experienced only in the moment, the world just happens.

The Human Object

We objectify our world and others in it. "Others," indeed! "[Eighteen-month-old children] mostly treat contemporaries as physical objects or disregard them completely. Five in one room may each disregard one of the others. If two were together near an object, one may just push the other out of the way impersonally, as though he were an object . . . one as [he] climbs, pushes a second, who falls on a third. All ignore this. Or two may try to climb up in exactly the same place. Both struggle with each other, but merely for the space, not aggressively, as later. Child wanting to sit on chair filled by other child may either sit *on* other child or may spill him out. May walk around or just bump into other child." (Ames.)

What a startling observation! So much skill has been acquired, so many lessons learned, and, yet, still no Other. No Self like you in all your world because you know no Self— you, the person, are not there—although your memory, thoughts, and sensations make up all the world.

Your unselfconscious will is in the service of acquiring. It is possessive and slow to emerge. At twelve months of life, about to walk, with words to say and understand: ". . . even the sense of personal possession is practically absent and he makes very meager distinctions between himself and others." (Gesell.) Possession comes late and precedes Self; possessive pronouns are used first. "Child grabbed from may hang onto object; and may let it go and cry; may just let it go; may shout 'mine.'" (Ames.) At twenty-four months of age, "Pronouns, *mine, me, you,* and *I,* are coming into use approximately in the order just given." (Gesell.) "Mine" leads to "me" (the object) and "you" (the object) and finally to "I," an "I" whose shape and meaning are ruled by the possessive mode.

4.

The Action Mode

When we see and when we think and walk and eat and breathe we serve ourselves, our purpose. The purpose guides the rest. In the beginning, floating in the maternal ocean, we allow the environment in and are nourished. Indeed, we should not say "allow." Allowing is an adult decision. In the womb we just exist in a state of permeation, perfused with the blood and vibrations of our world. Then, during the cataclysm of birth, we struggle for the first time. What had been a world of comfort is now pain, and we contract to shut it out, to gain control, to act and so to change the turbulence back to peace. With the first breath, and the first breast, peace does return. The infant body loosens, relaxing as the warmth flows in, allowing what is needed to enter once again, receptive to the world. In the early weeks all is intake, relaxation, sleep, and food. Briefly, however, between feeding and sleep, eyes focus on the world; they are active, following, reaching out in interest rather than in pain. The motive differs but the function is the same: to act upon the world. A mode of living has begun: life as acting on the world, doing things to all the objects of the object world so as to bring about possession and relief from pain.

The lessons, bottle, ball, mother, nose, are lessons in possession, in reaching for what is shiny, bright, warm, and safe. Name what's good and squeeze it with the fingers, draw it to the mouth, and take it in. The baby reaches for the bottle, eyes focused, brain intent, arms extended and waving with excitement. Into the mouth pops the nipple—and what a change! The body softens, eyes cross, lids droop down, arms relax. And then—sleep. All functions are eased, immersed back into a resting world. The action mode yields to the receptive mode, phasing back and forth. For a brief while, at the beginning, reception dominates the infant life. It will recede as we acquire the world.

School continues. More and more the action mode rules the day. With practice and reward it grows in scope until, with symbols, it creates thought to plan its action. Then thoughts detach from sensations, becoming self-sufficient, independent, and, finally, absolute. The abstract world is born; thoughts seem real. Memory builds a Past and imagination creates a Future; between both they establish Time. The action mode sets priorities: "mine, me, you,"—in that order we learn. Possession shapes the Self and the world.

As our bodies teach our minds so our minds instruct our bodies. Desire for the ball will focus eyes. The broad, impressionistic world narrows to a central stage whose sharp details and clear edges separate the ball from all the rest, which now recedes, vanishing into background. Muscles tense and capillaries shunt the blood from gut to muscles; adrenalin executes the change. Breathing hastens and the chest expands. Eyes and neck and body synchronize, directed to the target. Watching the ball roll, learning what it does, teaches object logic: A is not B. Object thought is born with the rolling ball. The ball, an object; the ball, a thought. They are linked together, welded tight, until our thought blankets our perception.

Thinking is for action, for acquisition and control. Thinking guides effort until thought itself is effortful. The knitted brow, the intent look, the tensing of the eyes, all partners to a single purpose, a mode of being in the world. "Me" and "you" and "I" are sharpened, suitable for object games. "Mine" is the favorite, and clear boundaries are the rule. Day by day, body and mind coordinate, learning control, learning to manipulate the world. The action mode becomes the norm. Reception, where we started, is used for sleep and food and comforting.

As conscious doing is the essence of the action mode, allowing is the essence of the receptive. With the action mode we divide and conquer our environment. With the receptive, we take in, receive and unify. It is the difference between breathing out and breathing in. Try a sample, now. Take a full breath; breathe in and then breathe out. Notice the difference in your state of mind during those two phases. On inhaling, mental contents become diffuse, thinking tends to stop. On exhaling, energy flows out, the vision sharpens; thinking, too, is sharper on exhalation, boundaries more clear.

When manifesting in the action mode, when striving in the world, the electrical currents of the brain are fast and short.

The big muscles tense and eyes focus; the sensual recedes. But in the receptive mode, the senses unfold. Vision softens, muscles relax, alpha waves may appear: slow, irregular, and higher waves, they indicate a change in attitude, something subtle, beyond words.

And words themselves, where do they belong? Our words are from the object world, the world we made by separation, in the action mode. Words are the tools of that mode. With them we discriminate, with them we divide reality into pieces, objects, things, which we can grab with minds or bodies. The Eskimo has many words for snow, the skier several, the average man just one—according to need, according to the word's function in the action mode. Although objects may have many names, sensations have very few, but not from the dullness of our perception. We can discriminate a thousand hues of color but not name them. Feelings are the same. How many forms of love have we to match against the one word? Love is experienced in the receptive mode. It is the action mode that separates with forms, boundaries, words, logic, and the Road of Time. The receptive mode unifies, is sensory and diffuse; receptive time is instantaneous, all at once. In that mode, the self merges into Now. What do you call relationships where A *is* B? I-Thou, Buber named it. I-It is in the action mode.

The function, the goal we set, controls the mode. What's the goal? Is it combat, control, and capture, or receive, synthesize, allow? It is not activity versus passivity. "Allowing" is an action but of a different kind. We say "I-It" and fire the bullet so it intersects the racing deer. We say "I-Thou" and receive our lover's embrace. We need both modes; each has its place and function. Merge with the infinite and you lose the deer. Calculate your "making love" and it becomes another task, depriving you of re-creation. Yet they can blend. You can work in your garden, uprooting the weeds, one by one, while being receptive to the breeze and the soft earth.

Infants and children must perform their biological task: survival in a biological world. That primary need begins in the womb and pervades the childhood years; it has trained us all too well in the action mode. The receptive comes occasionally, hardly at command, as if it were an alien being. That which should be familiar we come to perceive as strange. Years later, as adults, we may go to special schools to learn receiving, to regain the mode with which our life began. Until then, the receptive mode goes obsolete, latent, receding from the repertoire, but not forgotten.

> There was a time when meadow, grove, and stream,
> The earth and every common sight,
> To me did seem
> Apparelled in celestial light,
> The glory and the freshness of a dream. [Wordsworth.]

Glory? Not likely in the child. But when adults recover their receptive mode and grow to a new wholeness, recruiting to the soft, wide span of childhood vision the complex meanings of adult thought—then glory, then, perhaps, a dream transcending the dreams of one-eyed man.

5.

Consequences

Self, Time, Anxiety

The action mode creates a world. That world has dimensions of its own, distinctive features, normally unquestioned in their status as elemental facts. Who does not assume a separate self and the flow of Time? They are the pillars that uphold that world, but they were not given: they grew or were made.

The self grew, for the organism has its plan. We started as pure happening; we were what was occurring in the womb. With the birth process, intention formed to direct action: fear and desire took their roots, then grew in strength like other parts. With intention, the body self took form, for the body is the agent of intention and executes the biological plan: possession. (Mine, me, you, I—in that order.) The body is the source of pain and pleasure, qualities that dominate our sensory world. They are so compelling, they define what is "personal," what belongs to self. Their authority is never questioned.

Memory and symbol engage sensation, organizing objects and object laws. Others see your body as an object and that helps you do so, too.

"What a pretty smile you have!" "Come here!" "Wave your hand!"

The body possesses and possession is the game.

"Here is your bottle." "Give me the ball." "Want the doll?" What the body hugs belongs to self; what it does not touch may disappear.

First the ball, then the reaching arm, then the body of the arm, and then the reaching wish produces "me"—all objectified into the landscape of the object world, seen from a window. The window frames the world and in the space behind the window an invisible object forms: "I." Gradually, a solitary Self is born.

Memory creates Time and orders objects in a Past. Images and words create a Future, ordering the objects yet to come. Between the Past and Future, laws are found, connecting both in a smooth path on which walks the form of Self. Like a cage of tigers, the trained objects stiffen to the whip of logic and take their places in an even line, arrayed in demonstration of predictive power. Wild applause greets success, but when the noise subsides, another character appears: Anxiety. What if the tigers all jump down and in disordered rage make a bloody meal of the maestro? These shadows of the future, cast by the past, can overwhelm the bright display. The scene of gaiety and pride may give way to troubled dreams.

The action mode has welded past and future into an arrow. As it flies there can be no rest, for Now has disappeared.

Zeno's paradox is lived by us. By the action mode we acquire Self, gain power, and survive. But Past and Future, joined by Anxiety, has no room for Now. Scurrying in memory, images, and thought, we have no time to stop and be nourished by the world. A hunger grows: dissatisfaction. Forgetting how to eat, we begin to starve at the banquet. Believing what we're taught, we cannot fit the world.

More school, defining Self: boy, girl, good, bad, fast, slow, happy, sad, strong, weak, pretty, ugly, smart, and dumb. The Self stands like a sculptor's armature, and the others fire away, heaving globs of clay to spatter, stick, and lump together as the self-shape grows. "Tommy is a good boy with blond hair, a nice smile, smart and fast." "Jennie is a pretty girl, delicate and sweet, with brown hair, a merry laugh, and very understanding." "Jim is a roughneck, not too bright." "Helen has black hair and big feet; she's homely but kind." Animated sculptures taking shape, sitting in rows in school. Eyes peering out of the hardening clay.

Adolescence, we are told, is the time of identity. Teenagers intimately converse: "Who are you and who am I?" No wonder the question is asked. Awkwardly, the clay figures stagger around the room, trying to walk after such a difficult new birth.

"You tell me and I'll tell you." (Maybe we'll find out that way.) "You are really very sensitive!" (Not much help, just more clay.) Some rough places are smoothed and a hole or two filled in. Adult statues serve as guides and they so stiff they have forgotten what the young ones can still feel: that something doesn't fit. "It looks just fine!" (But it doesn't feel right.) The clay binds and cramps in all the wrong places. A memory of freedom haunts the room.

How Do You Spend Your Day?

On waking in the morning, things are unsorted. The first stumbling steps informed by a foggy vision give way to clear re-entry into the familiar. You wash your face, brush your teeth, enjoying without realizing it the sensations of your present moment. Before long, your thoughts begin: remembering, planning, drifting briefly into fantasy. Thoughts of the day's work, yesterday's events, wishes for the future, all perform an act of transmigration, and you fly through your breakfast world, only occasionally aware of the taste of the food and its texture, or the colors and light of the room. Your day of fantasy has begun.

The morning paper may complete the job. The same news you read yesterday, a day further along, absorbs attention with a thousand details, none vital, but all arousing concern, fear, and desire. It would not matter if you had been away for months, your newspaper would sound the same. If not the paper, then the radio, television, bringing the morning news, the weather, and the ads. A familiar noise—it fills the spaces between thought and memories.

So into the car or into the bus or train and go to work. Busses and trains hold rows of people at morning prayer, or so it seems, heads bowed over their texts, swaying together in silent, somber attention. Inside those heads the movie film unwinds. A few pairs of eyes look out the window, some seeing, some in dreamland.

Finally, the job. Absorption in a task is some relief—and even satisfaction. But symbolic satisfactions set the pace. Victories of effort allay fear, promote pride, provide assurance of control and worth. Success means all the dreams will turn out fine, all the fantasies and images are warm and bright. The thousand faces of the Other, mounted on swivel necks, in neutral position while the issue is in doubt, at the moment of success swing toward you with smiles and admiration. You rest a while, savoring the glow, but it does not last long. The heads soon swing back to neutral, threatening, should you falter, to swing the other way and be transformed into a crowd of departing strangers.

Yet a task is good; it may demand you focus your attention, eliminating thoughts and images as you exercise skill, immersed in the process.

The effort continues, tiredness ensues, and then—lunch, usually a social event. With the others you can talk and laugh, without demands. But did you taste your lunch?

Back to work—wrestling with the future in the landscape of your phantom mind. During the day, if you were lucky, a brief suspension of concern and will took place. Your energies flowed, converging on the task; and with just the lightest touch to guide the stream, something whole emerged, new to you, not exactly yours. The creative moment was complete; it filled you, solid, there. You felt its difference from all the rest, its flowing life, that magical appearance of something more than you—from you.

But that moment may not come today, or for many days.

The housewife is the same. The morning cleanup, helped perhaps by radio or television. Live a thousand fantasies while the vacuum cleaner sucks up dirt, its noise washing out detail. The dishes done in reverie, the grocery list prepared, the washer filled. And in the afternoon, perhaps a gathering of friends for talk and stimulation in the abstract world. What was the texture of the cup? What was the feeling in the eyes that touched briefly?

The end of day, at home again where everyone converges with his or her hunger, not just for food. Man, woman, and child gather there to receive, for so much effort wants reward. Husband and wife greet each other to be filled; so do the children. The supper meal, biggest of the day, designed to fill, can give some joy if not washed under by the daydreams or the talk. Then television, the paper, cards, or a gathering of friends for talk, for words and concepts, memories, private thoughts. Finally, sleep. Perhaps sex before sleep, a touching and a sensing of what is Now, but much entangled in the will. Concepts, planning intrude on sex; doing, rather than allowing, may be the mode, and in the doing fantasies take part, instructions from the latest book: "Fantasies are good. Remember all the zones—take your time—relax—don't worry." Is she ready? Should I tell him? Sex can become another task, prior to sleep, but mixed with satisfaction, still. The charge of body energy brings you home for a moment, dissolving the structures of the mind and leaving in its wake peace and joy—a little. Not often, perhaps. Indeed, sometimes never.

Then sleep. For some, a pill to gain control, even here. The drug most used in all our land is a tranquilizer.

The weekend. Work around the house. Go to a restaurant, to eat without demands. The service and the expectations are more important than the food. Relief, indeed. Perhaps a movie. Three hours of symbols, fantasies, emotions, nothing you have to do but surrender to someone else's world. Afterward, let's be social: talk, anxiety, alcohol, and games. That loving feeling underneath emerging for a moment, now and then.

Then, religion, dependency fulfilled. A contract, sure enough, for work performed, for control, for faithfulness, the promise of eternal care. Father and mother fantasies above the clouds, accompanied by organs and emotion, and singing all together for the comfort of the group. Yet an echo of something else may pervade the hall. Something may be touched, some reminder. "Oh yes, I must come more often." Out into the day, for greetings, talk, and home.

Perhaps sports, pure play (unless a task). Performance measured by the number may spoil that, too, but there are times when the miraculous happens. The body flows into the ball, the skis, the wave, and once again a light turns on. "Oh yes! I had forgotten—I want more." You forget again, the memory drowned out by all that's different. Sports may mean to watch, in stadium or on television, giving oneself up to another dream. At the end you are elated by a vicarious victory or angered by defeat but, either way, a little drained, a little fuzzy in the head: the sign of fantasy.

All this may seem extreme, an exaggeration for poetic

style. You and I are not like that, not living in a phantom world of abstract symbols, strung together into an enormous net with a mesh so fine that as it covers up the world hardly a speck shows through. "Not me!" Are you sure?

Consider: Every thought you have is unreal. Each one is an abstraction, a shadow of the thing that is. Your future is not real (imagine a purple cow). Your past is not real, for the past is memories. (How can you fit your memory of the ocean inside your living room?) Memories are images of where you are not, so how can the past be real? Concepts are not real. Write "One million dollars" on a paper and take it to your grocer. Good luck. Thinking is not real. It's a tool. Would you lay a loaf of bread upon a scale, then eat the scale? *Bon appétit!* Every thought you have is unreal, every memory you have is unreal, every imagining you have is unreal, all your anxieties are unreal, all your hopes are unreal, all your desires. All that which you remember having, all that which you imagine will come—all are unreal. So what of the day that you just lived in fantasy—in abstraction, concerned with past pleasures and future problems—how much was real?

"All this is crazy; you go too far. It's semantics, tricks with words—that's all!"

Have you ever noticed how they do the news whenever a war is on? Do you remember those reports? "Fifty-five enemy soldiers killed!" They didn't say, "Fifty-five husbands, brothers, lovers, fathers, sons were killed today by our efforts." Curious, isn't it? "Fathers" evokes the real. "Enemy soldiers" evokes a dream. If we evoked the real, what would happen then? Consider. Billions of your dollars go for war. You are not the only one. Billions of Russian rubles go for war. Billions of your dollars go for killing a husband, a father, a brother, a lover—or defending yourself against Them doing that to you.

Our resources are ending, that is true. We take the dwindling energies and precious metals and fashion machines to destroy cities that we will be unable to rebuild. Working hard, creatively and well, we have accumulated bombs and poisons in such vast quantities that their use would destroy all life. We breed viruses never seen before; their military potential is truly staggering. To minister to our fantasies, to entertain us, we give to a man or woman a hundred times the money we give to him who grows our food. There is not enough food, but more babies are produced. We are poisoning what we breathe and what we drink and what we eat. We are waiting.

It is the nature of ideas and fantasies and symbols that they have no guiding wisdom of their own. The action mode is out of control, and we are dreaming a symbolic world, only briefly waking to what is real.

At the same time (in the nick of time?), if we are lucky we are stirred to a saving action, for as we grow older our fantasies of power may lose their credibility. Death approaches and the dissatisfaction that gnawed from time to time now mixes with anxiety and causes us to look around for a way out. Activities and fantasies will not do. What else is there? Where, in all this enormous room, is there a door?

6.

Spiritual Doors

The mystical, spiritual, religious life has always been here. From the corner of your eye you saw the churches and processions, you read of "holy men" and fat Zen beggars full of enlightenment. Western scientists have proved that meditation rests the body, but yogis have been chanting mantras for three thousand years. From India, China, Japan, Arabia come strange tales of strange people hinting persistently that there exists a way. For Christians, there's the image of cowled monks, a cross, and Saint Teresa. "Lord Jesus Christ, have mercy on me"—the West has mantras, too. Western meditation is called "affective prayer" and "contemplation," and asceticism is nothing new. It's all in our tradition, but few think of it as a door. Religion mostly isn't. Crusades in many forms kill for Christ, or in the name of Allah or a Hindu god. Yet the texts go back three thousand years and the men who wrote them do not seem like fools. For example: Buddha.

Old age, sickness, and death—these were what the young Buddha saw when he was not the Buddha but Siddhartha

Gautama, a prince with wealth, a beautiful wife, and a young child. Old age, sickness, and death. He realized those three things could affect him, too, even though he was a prince and the sun shone on him. Dissatisfaction with his life suddenly flowered at that moment, and he abandoned his royal way of life to seek an end to his dissatisfaction, an end to the anxiety that these realities aroused in him. Six years later, he said he found it. Not through mortifying his body, although he did that, not through living as a hermit in the forest, although he did that, and not through practicing the special meditations through which he achieved strange states of consciousness. He did learn from all these things, but what he learned was that they were of no use, their effects didn't last. Time after time, Gautama must have found himself still back at the human position, still dissatisfied, still anxious about the prospect of old age, disease, and death. So he gave up. He gave up his efforts, he gave up his austerities, and he gave up his disciples—the ones who came to him because of the fame of his self-mortifications. He sat under a tree, for there was nothing else to do. It is said that in that state of cessation of striving he gazed upon the morning star and was enlightened as to Truth. This Truth set him free—free from suffering, from dissatisfaction.

There were Buddhas before Gautama and Buddhas after him, Buddhas in the West as well as in the East, men and women who found a way and a door—or so they said—and left instructions for others to do the same. The instructions haven't been a great success; the world seems as bloody-minded now as it ever was, and Buddhas are not numerous.

Yet so many Buddhas point to the same door we would be foolish to pass it by. At least we can understand what they are talking about even if we decline to go that way.

"If we keep ourselves free from the things that are outside us, God will give us in exchange everything that is in heaven . . . itself with all its powers." (Meister Eckhart.) "Binding the mind stuff to a place is fixed attention . . . focusedness of the presented idea on that place is contemplation. . . ." (Patanjali.) "When this active effort of mental concentration is successful, it is followed by a more passive, receptive state of samadhi in which the earnest disciple will enter into the blissful abode of noble wisdom." (Goddard.) "For if such a soul should desire to make any effort of its own with its interior faculties, this means that it will hinder and lose the blessings which . . . God is instilling into it and impressing upon it." (Hilton.)

These are instructions for you, instructions in opening a door, the "spiritual" door. They are very interesting instructions if you notice that they are basically the same, even though they come from men who spoke quite different languages, lived centuries apart, and went their own way. The instructions can be summed up simply: practice "renunciation" and "meditation."

Renunciation. There's a heavy word! All those images of self-denial: the wild-haired, skinny, bearded old man in the desert cave; the beautiful nun hidden away, entombed within convent walls; flagellations of the body and the spirit—we confuse means and ends. There is another definition of renunciation: "Renunciation . . . is not giving up the things of this world, it is accepting that they go away." (Suzuki.) Allowing, letting, nonattachment: renunciation means relaxing the grasping hand—the opposite of the action mode. Have you ever done it? Have you ever quit, really taken a vacation? How hard it is to stop! In the national parks the visitors stream from busses, cameras ready, kids in hand, naming the flowers and the trees, stunned for a moment by the first view but soon hard at work looking and doing. All the while, the mountains stand there waiting to speak if the noise would just die down. Sometimes it does. Sometimes one person's mind, blessed by fatigue or sudden shock, just stops; his eyes are open, he is listening, and the world comes in. That's meditation. That's contemplation. That's renunciation: when you stop. The door is not "religious," not exotic, full of incense, robes, and symbols. It is not alien, not strange, not secret—just unpracticed. Buddha taught: "One is one's own refuge, who else could be the refuge?" "He said that there was no esoteric doctrine in his teachings, nothing hidden in the 'closed fist' of the teacher." (Rahula.) Nothing hidden, nothing secret— just forgotten.

Perhaps you don't believe me. Perhaps you grew up thinking meditation meant crossing your legs, chanting Sanskrit, fingering beads, looking holy, or just being a freak. Enlightenment meant your troubles were gone, you could fly through the air, read minds, and avoid reincarnation as a frog. Spiritual meant religion: bishops and rabbis, solemn-faced priests and ministers, and an endless line of organs playing hush-and-glory music. Okay, but set all that aside for a while. Let's go to a monastery and see what actually goes on. Monasteries are schools where you learn to be "spiritual." Perhaps we can understand what they do, and why.

In mid-California, some twenty miles inland from the Big Sur coast, is Tassajara, a Zen monastery. It was a hot-springs resort, so it doesn't look like Shangri-La. Everyone in it is American and rather young. Yet it's very Japanese. The gateway entrance is traditional, and time is regulated by the notes of bells and wood clappers resonating impressively through the quiet air. The men and women wear black robes, and the men, and some women, shave their heads—definitely exotic. And when you look in at the zendo (the meditation hall), you see them sitting in cross-legged rows like a picture out of the *National Geographic*. The students are doing "zazen" meditation. They have been told to follow their breathing or to count their breaths one by one and not to get involved in thinking or daydreaming. They are instructed to keep their backs straight and breathe from the belly. Pacing slowly along the rows is a robed figure carrying a stick, and every now and then one of the seated students presses his palms together, bows forward, and gets whacked on the shoulder. Strange indeed! They do that for forty minutes at a time and then get up, walk slowly around the hall, sit down, and do it again.

The students have their meals in the zendo, too; the diet is vegetarian. Mealtime is more ceremony than eating, full of wrapping and unwrapping bowls, placing spoons and chopsticks in ritual order, and chanting verses in Japanese. Sometimes, in the evening, there is a lecture about Zen. It's philosophical, in English, full of paradoxes, usually a translation of everyday events into Buddhism.

> There are perhaps three kinds of creation. The first is to be aware of ourselves after we finish zazen. When we sit we are nothing, we do not even realize what we are; we just sit. But when we stand up, we are there! That is the first step in creation. When you are there, everything else is there; everything is created all at once. When we emerge from nothing, when everything emerges from nothing, we see it all as a fresh new creation. This is non-attachment.
> [Suzuki.]

Try zazen. If you sit cross-legged for forty minutes you will get pains in your legs. The students are told, "Be the pain, watch it, don't move, don't complain, accept it." If the student is disappointed with his meditation, he may be told, "You have a gaining idea in mind." Thinking, daydreams, and emotions are described as intrusions, as distractions to be patient with until they go away. The student should not strive for enlightenment, he is told, because if he is truly "just sitting" he is enlightenment itself. The person meditating is not supposed to do anything except *be* sitting. "Be" is sensory-perceptive, concrete.

Like monasteries of other systems, Tassajara is a communal society. Although there are some status rewards, there are certainly no profits in the monetary sense. The work is shared in rotation, and the daily routine has little variety to it. Each activity is represented as being equally important as any other; washing dishes is supposed to be as "good" as walking in the woods.

There are no televisions, no radios, no movies. Three times a year, there is a week of intensive meditation called sesshin, in which the students spend seven days sitting in meditation in the zendo from before dawn to late at night. Occasionally, they have an interview with the Zen master.

That's it. Tassajara is a Japanese Zen Buddhist monastery sitting in the mountains of California, attended by young Americans. What does it mean? Assuming there's something to it, what is that something? How do we make sense out of it? What does it contribute and what are its limitations? One cannot judge too well from the outside, but an interesting consistency emerges when one thinks of the rituals as techniques pursuant to a goal: teaching the receptive mode.

To begin with, zazen, "just sitting," is the opposite of everything we have learned to do. We learned to move our minds from sensation to thought. In infancy we were an arm reaching for a spot of color. The muscle and the color became one. Over and over again we reached until we saw only an object, the ball, and we saw the shape before the color. Finally there was only the ball and we hardly felt the reaching of our arm; it had become automatic. Our minds were free to think ahead and know where the ball would land. We learned to move and see and hear and touch automatically, freeing energy for thought. Now we can think and be only half aware of sight and touch and sound: thought dominates our conscious life. But when we meditate, what are we doing? It doesn't matter if it's a yogic, Zen, or Christian form. The meditation de-automatizes the generation of our thoughts by sending us back along the developmental path: sensations receive our attention while thought is ignored; the attention energy withdrawn from abstractions is reinvested in perception. Breathing, chanting, saying mantras, or "just sitting," the focus is the same: sensation.

Whereas the action mode controls, the receptive mode allows—and meditation is allowing. Hour after hour, sitting in the zendo, the students learn the receptive mode, the one they started with but set aside and now, belatedly, renew. True, it's very exotic, very mysterious, very Japanese. Fundamentally, however, it's a functional matter. They didn't wear wristwatches in medieval Japan, so they had bells and wooden blocks they struck with mallets. But they still use them. Clocks and watches would stimulate minds into the Western mode. Bells and chimes are better. The penetrating sound stops thought and hangs there, shimmering, teaching the mind to follow it into silence. Long robes slow you down; a deep bow stops you. The ritual at mealtime receives full attention, and silence helps shift our organismic program from the abstract future to the sensory now. Linear time, the pillar of our usual world, is undermined by hours of sitting and counting breaths, by the merging of one day into the next through unvarying routine, by lectures convincing intellects that their intellect is wrong.

The gospel preached aims at your motivation. Our motives program our perception; our purpose organizes our world. So acquisition is the first to go, the primary purpose of the action mode. The self is fired at by sermons teaching ego is illusion, by standardizing clothes and posture, work, and meals, by minimizing speech. Death, the focus of an anxious life, is discredited, declared to be a product of delirious minds. Pain, the prod that taught us boundaries and motivations, is challenged and dismissed in meditation. You are told to "be the pain" and keep on sitting. "Endure, don't run; experience, accept!" Pleasure, too, must lose appeal, lose its beckoning power, to bring about the shift in mode. If you "accept," "let go," and never seek the memory of the past, how can pleasure serve to guide your acts? So open your hand. "Renunciation is not giving up the things of this world; it is accepting that they go away."

And when, in sesshin, you sit for seven days counting breaths, following sensations, it does its job. The stoutest defender of the action mode will waver somewhere in those seven days. The carrot of enlightenment is dangled before the goal-seeking mind, dangled forever out of reach, yielding in the end frustration and moments of collapse of mode.

It's all scientific, planned. There can be more to it, of course; there probably is; certainly at one time there was. The monastery was a tool, an instrument to help in opening an unseen door; it had a function once, in a certain country, at a certain time. From the outside it's hard to tell what's happening now, but this pattern, at least, can be seen: the monastery works to shift the organism's plan—from control, manipulation (the action mode) to allowing, receiving (the receptive).

You see, there is nothing "mystical" here at all; it could be done by other means, without robes, without sutras, without the lotus position and the rice and bowls. After all, if you are Japanese, it isn't exotic to be chanting Japanese, or sitting cross-legged eating rice, or bowing fifty times a day. Indeed, what we need now may not be something from a foreign country which existed in an alien time.

The religious monasteries understood their tools quite well, when they began. In western lands we have a training, too, where students sit in a small space, confined to concentrate on dull, repeated stimuli, restrained from movement hour after hour, reciting texts of gospel. We call them public schools. Their original purpose was to turn out scribes, clerk machines for the upper class. They're changing now, but we have our purpose and means confused and don't quite understand the mode we use.

7.

Other Doors

If you were a yogi, would it be different? "The Truth of Atman is revealed when a qualified aspirant instructed by an illumined teacher practices the disciplines of self-control, meditation, and inwardness of mind." (*The Upanishads.*) Not much different. Some paths devote you to a guru or a god. What sort of "refuge in one's self" is that? But the texts go on to say, "Worship the guru until you know the guru is yourself." "I am God," said Hallaj. Dependency is turned around, merging the parent and the child until the human being stands forth.

Renunciation, acceptance, selflessness, the notes are played on different instruments but yield a similar melody: Change your goal and your world changes. Change your inner attitude, change the purpose of your life.

You see, it's a functional matter. Body-mind obeys your commands. Set your goals to act, acquire, or fight, and lo! Time is born, enabling prediction. Symbols fill awareness, creating plans, giving meaning to an abstract future. A self is built to focus and reflect the plan. Fear and Pain assume command, adjusting your response. Vision sharpens on strategic forms. The incidental drops away; the sensual is set aside so the target can be clear.

Now change the goal, shift to Being. Receive the world and be nourished. The gaze will soften, vision diffuse, maximizing entry of the sensate world. Time dissolves and Now emerges, accompanied by satisfaction. The Self subsides and the world enters. Muscle tension eases, breathing slows, judgments fall away. Beyond fear, beyond pleasure, Now *is*. All questions are answered—for the questions have disappeared; they are the product of another mode, the action mode, another world. The mode of Being, the receptive mode, serves a different function. It is not "higher," not more "spiritual"—just breathing in instead of breathing out. Half a breath cycle is not enough. We need both to live. We need both modes.

You didn't have to learn to breathe, your body knew how. It knows the way to another world, too. Those moments happen all the time, without a monastery, and you don't call them spiritual, but you probably think of them as special. They are. Specially desirable, pleasurable, motivating you for a brief time to try to stay with it, come back to it, have it more. If you play golf, they are the moments when you let the club hit the ball and just watch, transfixed by the perfect flight following the perfect, easy swing. In tennis, pressed to the limit, running full tilt, you whip your body into the ball with a smooth, complete, unthought motion, and the ball flashes across the court for the point. You couldn't repeat it if you tried, particularly if you tried. Skiing, basketball, running—it doesn't matter—there are those times when you go "beyond yourself" and "something else" takes over, transforming all to smoothness, delight, and performance "above your head." There are books now that you can read, showing sports as something more than play, recreation in the original sense, perhaps.

Sex will do it. If love is there, enough tenderness to make your partner real, you may become a flow that takes you "out of yourself" and carries you someplace from which you later know you have returned. Drugs can do it for a while, even alcohol sometimes provides a foggy feeling of an opening door, but as drugs wear off the door slams shut again, and it may be harder afterward to return, and harder still to live the vision in your daily world. Church can do it but it's very hard, since you are so flooded with emotion and all that canned music from the choir. With saints and sinners, bad paintings, and boring talks, it's a miracle the door can open at all. But it can, for true devotion can change the inner program. Service will do it: the performance of an action because it needs to be done—not for gain, not for reward, not for anything except itself, just doing it. Just doing is meditation.

Creative work is a door for many. To be creative, you've got to stop, to lay off, to sit back a bit, to take your chance and let the thing flow. No matter if you're writing, composing, building a house, teaching a child, cooking a meal, there's something in us that does it better than we can consciously do, and when it happens we are satisfied. Satisfied because it's so complete; there's nothing else to want.

So it isn't just big moments, great discoveries that you read about in books, with inventor/mystics leaping wildly to their feet, spouting verse and ecstasy. It can be something small, something no one else would know or notice: the movement of a hand in setting three flowers in a glass, or the instantaneous and smooth turning of the wheel that slides your car across an icy road to safety.

But you're not a saint, you're like a child with a bicycle who gets it going for half a second, then lands on his head. The moments are too infrequent and the range too narrow. The self dies hard; it hovers in the background even when we think it's gone. We take that special moment and cash it in to keep on playing our usual game. "Wow! That was great! If I could do that often, I'd be the star, I'd earn a lot of money, I'd win the Nobel Prize—and all those women [or all those men]." "Spiritual materialism" infests the land like a strain of virus combining the common cold with athlete's foot. We're the carrier. But, still, we have our moments and in those moments, during that split second, or make it two or three, you're in a different place, tantalizing in its promise of something wonderful that is always there.

In those moments you become No-Self. You haven't disappeared, you've not gone anywhere, nor has the world, but it's different. The fantasies are gone, the symbols are not there, the net that has covered all the world has been removed and you are free—whatever it is you are. Unlike the world of self, there is nothing to be added, nothing to be done, nothing incomplete. At that moment the world is you and you're it. Enlightenment? Not yet. But it's a step through a door; so congratulations, John Doe—you're a mystic now and then.

8.

Dependency

Now and then is not enough, and that way is a door, not a destination. Realizing that, you may decide you need to go to school; you ask around, applying to the one that sounds the best. Looking for help, being ignorant as hell, you jump in, sign up, and take the vows—whatever they may be. Then, full of hope, you pack your bags and off you go to school, to spiritual school, to be enlightened.

Unfortunately, you took along (unawares) a stowaway. Between the underwear and the toothbrush, your old companion sneaked aboard and went along: dependency.

Spiritual schools are for the dependent, too. Prayers and mantras, lots of kneeling, robes, incense, and relics—magic to summon power from the Big One to make you immortal, unafraid, blissful forever. Dependency-greed finds a home: "Satchitananda! I'm told the chicks in the ashrams get pretty horny after a while and it's good hunting. But if you hold off on the sex, you can get a really big orgasm they call enlightenment. It's far out! And I kind of like the Sufi dancing—it really gets me high. Did you get zapped by Muktananda? He's better than Guru Maharaji. See you around! Have a good one!"

Spiritual schools are still schools and schools have teachers and teachers become parents to learners who become children. "One is one's own refuge; who else could be the refuge?" said the Buddha, but all the eager heads, mouths open, nod in admiration and reverent wonder—then swallow it down, open their mouths again and wait for more. "To study Buddhism is to study the self. To study the self is to forget the self. To forget the self is to be enlightened by the ten thousand dharmas. . . ." (Dogen.) "Yes, yes! Tell us more!" Mouths open . . . waiting.

The list of the seven deadly sins has left out the worst one. For if you want to know reality and act in it with your creative power, dependency will do you in. Perhaps it's not listed because it's so often hidden and has so occupied our perception that we are not aware of how tyrannically it binds our lives. What we are told is dependency is a caricature: the man or woman still tied to the mother's apron strings or dominated by a spouse. Dependency is more subtle and disguised than that: it is just the wish to have parents.

Dependency is a fantasy. In that fantasy parents know what you should do; they give you what you want and what you need. They are powerful. With their power, parents can control what you cannot: love, anger, and fear; sickness, age, and death. They give attention and esteem and love you no matter what you do. They make no demands—except submission. Parents will provide if you bend your knee. In dependency, tyranny is sought, not overthrown; for the more tyranny, the more comfort in the parents' power.

Who are the parents of our adult years? Anyone will do. Husband, wife, son, daughter, boss, America, city hall. Neighbors, policeman, the company, the bar. Doctor, lawyer, senator, judge. The President of the United States of America. We all kneel.

Dependency is a disease, an insidious fantasy of protective power looking down, guarding you, judging you, rewarding you, punishing you. The disease has symptoms: helplessness, envy, vanity, jealousy, and admiration; blaming, exploitation, and reproach. "You're supposed to love me no matter what I do, for I've done my part [submission, feeling small and frightened], now you do yours!" Consider the justified anger, the sweet despair, the mournful longing, and the upward gaze, or the sullen pout that says, "I can't do it, I have no choice. You're supposed to do it, so give me what I need!" And when the fantasy seems true, when parents play their role just right, you're "blissed-out" with "God" or "life" or anything at all.

Perhaps you thought you left all that behind you when you left your home for college, job, or marriage. Not likely. Remember the moment when you said good-bye? You didn't really. Let me sketch the scene as, psychologically, it really was—and still may be, now.

The local band is playing outside, children, dogs and the ice-cream man, noisy in the street. The whole neighborhood is gathered, cheering with a banner: "Good luck to you! Come back and see us some time!"

Inside the house, the moment has come. Mother and Father

are standing there, tearful and proud. The suitcases are packed
and ready by the door. The rest of the family gathers around.
You kiss them all and shake their hands, embrace Mom and
Dad one last time. The band strikes up the final number, you
pick up your bags, open the door, and then march—round
and round the living room!

The band is gone, the street is quiet. Mom and Dad have
gone to bed. But chances are, you are still there, marching
around the living room of your childhood home.

It's very difficult to leave—and yet we must. Dependency
is so commercial; it's nothing but transactions from morn to
night. Security agreements, barter, bribes, and threats, manipulation and maneuvers of a hundred kinds. And all that ac-
counting and the double set of books, the strong-arm squad
collecting debts, for in dependency the parents can't say no,
they must pay up, there is no dropping out of the parent game.
Your own task is clear: bind the parent person and lock the
door. Once you've got the parent caught, he or she must be
fed; he must be satisfied to play the game. Yet it isn't that easy
to detect his needs, to give him what he wants so you'll get
yours. You must be good at watchfulness and care, with one
eye guarding the inner road on which your energy may flow.
Guard that road, for the unrestricted outflow of yourself may
take a form unpleasing to the Big One. You see, it's not an
easy business, living in dependency. It costs a lot.

Then are you never to be cared for? Are you never to relax, let go in the arms of lover, friend (or the world itself),
feeling cared for, at peace? Of course you can, such letting
go needs no fantasy and no parent—only trust: trust in your-

self, that your need will end, that you will want to work again and care for others, that your emptiness can be filled; trust in others, that they receive in the act of giving, that they need you to need them. It is an inward process through which you turn to others, *as they are,* to receive that which you must have. You do not need parents now, and you do not have them (as you had them then, or wanted them to be). To resurrect parents requires fantasy, and the price of fantasy is high.

You pay with fear. Pretending you are helpless, imagining you are small, feeling needy for protection, you scare yourself. It's part of the game, to be afraid. And having summoned parents, you become more fearful, for you harbor treason: wishes for the parents' power, anger at the parents' needs, resentment of the role of humbleness you must adopt. The treason is concealed but it poisons trust, creating loneliness.

You pay with greed. The child is needy, and feeling needy, in want of something from outside, how reasonable to seek possessions, love and power, money, sex and food. But the fantasy of needfulness turns pleasure into possession and power into tyranny. The acquisitions are symbolic: A millionaire will seek more millions, beyond consumption, for the emptiness will not be filled and the desire for security is not appeased. That hunger can consume the world, yet the appetite stays sharp. So your greed whips you on: to acquire clothes for vanity, thus building loneliness; to acquire homes for grandeur, in which you feel smaller.

You pay with vanity. You must be special and attractive in your body or your mind to catch the eye and hold the person who must save you. It's competition to the death, to win the prize from all the others. Fame entices in the hope that all-out war will capture entire populations of providers. And if you win? The people crowding toward you have dead eyes; they are blind, grasping, dependent, and self-centered. Throwing their own ropes of fantasy, they tie you to the book, performance, reputation—whatever object you have created. You have summoned angels to provide and find yourself with vampires that feed their own vanity by possessing you. In consolation, they leave piles of money on the floor. You gather it up thinking money means more pleasure, except that pleasure done too often fades away; and so you find, instead, the death of pleasure.

It is as if we saw the enormous animals of sickness, age, and death roaming wild across our land. Grasping power and fame like a bit and bridle in our sweating hands, we go chasing madly to fit them over the terrifying muzzles. But the animals are too big; they cannot be controlled. Sickness, age, and death tower over us, gigantic, while we scurry on hands and knees to harness their shadows.

So the house becomes emptier than when you began. That emptiness is born of your abstractions, and the fantasy of emptiness engenders fear. Fear drives you to the Future, and the satisfaction of the Now recedes and further disappears. Rising in its place are more abstractions, more desires, jealousies, envy, more vanity—more hungry ghosts rioting in the shadowy house within which you march around the deserted living room.

Dependency exacts a further price: it murders creativity.

Creative action plays with the unknown. But as the child fears the dark, full of big dogs and mental monsters formed from fantasies, the adult child will be fearful, too, faced with the dark world of the unknown mind, with vast concepts looming enormous just beyond the front yard. Peering out, he sees no parents in the darkness of that land where he has never been. The unknown is uncontrolled—no strategies exist that will enclose the endless territory of the new. Only trust in yourself and in this world can carry you past the watchdogs of your fears and out of the iron gates of the already-known. Dependency locks you in, secure.

In order to create, you must move forward into what you cannot see and urge it into being. You cannot do that in submission, doing what you're told—nor, in rebellion, not doing what you're told. In both, the focus is the same: turned back to Them. To be dependent, you stay a child. To stay a child, you stop reality's forward motion, roll back to a past time and freeze it there, preserved forever. It's "transference," the reliving of the past in the midst of the present, the casting of all newcomers into the roles of the dead. Time stands still, stagnant. When transference is finally given up, a person mourns the departing ghosts, who slip back into their proper graves, leaving that person "alone"—in the world—Now. But while the wax museum holds sway, nothing new can enter. Information needed for creation is made to pass a censor, whose job is preservation. Thus the past is reinforced to keep Now from flowing, for the flow will carry your parents away.

So to keep a fantasy, do not peer too closely at the world;

fuzzy vision suits you best. Your creative power, turned away, is aimed inside to juggle fantasies, to solve the problems of a child's intrigue. Thus, "What am I? Who am I?" the cardinal questions of our life, are never asked. These guiding questions direct creation in a thousand cultures; they are the points by which we navigate our voyage, carrying us as far as we will leave the land. They do not orient our lives in dependency. Aborted in its course, the creative thrust misses the world.

Dependency kills us, for it is the unknown that gives us life. The unknown flowers when we are receptive to it, allowing it to enter. The unknown carries us to the constantly forming edge of the world where light, beauty, and ecstasy are found. There is no other path to the spiritual, to the creative, to reality.

THE STORY OF THE CAPE

A woman came to Rabbi Israel, the maggid of Koznitz, and told him, with many tears, that she had been married a dozen years and still had not borne a son. "What are you willing to do about it?" he asked her. She did not know what to say. "My mother," so the maggid told her, "was aging and still had no child. Then she heard that the holy Baal Shem was stopping over in Apt in the course of a journey. She hurried to his inn and begged him to pray she might bear a son. 'What are you willing to do about it?' he asked. 'My husband is a poor bookbinder,' she replied, 'but I do have one fine thing that I shall give to the rabbi.' She went home as fast as she could and fetched her good cape, her 'Katinka,' which was carefully stowed away in a chest. But when she returned to the inn with it, she heard that the Baal Shem had already left for Mezbizh. She immediately set out after him and since she had no money to ride, she walked from town to town with her 'Katinka' until she came to Mezbizh. The Baal Shem took the cape and hung it on the wall. 'It is well,' he said. My mother walked all the way back, from town to town, until she reached Apt. A year later, I was born."

"I, too," cried the woman, "will bring you a good cape of mine so that I may get a son."

"That won't work," said the maggid. "You heard the story. My mother had no story to go by." [Buber.]

The creative life finds its own path.

In the Eastern disciplines, in the old times, you might have sat for days before the monastery gates or, having entered, failed another test and been sent away. Many were called, but few were chosen. Why? "Be free from greed!" "Be humble!" "Have courage!" How? In all the Vedas there are only exhortations: to meditate, to be sincere, to lead the virtuous life. But how? "Do not grasp!" But why do I grasp? Why is it so hard to let go? Self-reliance is essential, say the texts: "One is one's own refuge; who else could be the refuge?" Why do I look to the guru, instead of inside?

In the West, we have some understanding of our own. We have a science of psychology and have learned of motivation and defense. We can provide help for the disqualified. We understand that opening the fist is more complex than sobering a drunken monkey.

No external role can free us from dependency. It can

adapt to any form. The explorer in the arctic or the sailor on his solo trip across seven seas may still be voyaging in the world of his childhood, watched and applauded by giants in the sky. Dependency is inside, hidden in motivations. It is supported by belief in the badness of one's being, by fear of the wishes and emotions we sense bubbling potently in some inner volcano. We mistrust the natural energy and are convinced we must control it. Otherwise, it seems, the universe would take reprisal if we were unbound. Fearing ourselves, we fear the world and search for parents to control us and It and Them.

When we are young, our parents cause us pain, inevitably. To master this and maintain hope, we manufacture meaning as best we can. But the meaning we construct has only two compartments: good and bad. "Are they, my parents, bad?" That's a castastrophic thought, for parents are the world, and what hope can I maintain if the world is bad? "Am I bad?" That brings the hope that badness may be controlled, for if it's me that's bad, it lies within the circle of my will. So the badness that I felt without, I take within, and make into myself. Internalization, it is called. Anxiety is calmed, but the price is great. Assault from the outside mobilizes anger to repel the threat. When the enemy is outside, that anger can be released. When the internalizing choice is made—"I am the bad one"—the anger is entrapped and breeds mistrust of self. From the cauldron of that anger, demons emerge and monsters stalk the cellars of our mind. We grow into maturity watchful of misshapen creatures locked in secret rooms within. Let go, indeed! The legend of Pandora's box bespeaks our answer. We'll let go, all right, down to the first floor, perhaps. As for the depths beneath—the key stays in our pocket.

The hidden anger is denied, then "projected" back to the outside world, onto safer targets. Paranoia is our basic tool, transplanting the dangerous from us to Them. A hostile world is created by our anger and by the misinterpretations of the past. Who then can trust the world? One needs parents, allies, armies. Imagine this scene. Sunday at the beach: skywriting against a blue sky, a small plane glints in the sunlight, wheeling and diving. Its white path forms expanding letters and one by one they spell the words, "You need no one to take care of you." The statement shimmers in the air, viewed by the crowds below in utter disbelief and rage. "The world is full of murderous wolves!" they shout en masse. "We need a leader, to protect us from the sharp teeth!" Dependency thrives on fear and hostile vision. The child clings to the parent and will not let go.

"Letting go" means giving up control, allowing something else to be in charge. In any person it requires trust, but trust may be withheld. We know reasons why. The shock of being born, the transformation of a world of peace into suffocating chaos, may root distrust. The infant's world so open and so helpless cannot be free from trauma, and pain will raise suspicions of an evil force that needs to be controlled. The urge to master, to control, ensures our biological life; it is trained and reinforced in all our different schools. The first control is ordering sensations by selecting some and blocking out the rest. Then, control of body, control of objects; acquisition and defense become the master plan. Success produces parents' smiles; there are frowns for failure. Objects, persons, urine, feces, walking, eating, all, we learn, should be controlled, for helplessness invites disaster.

When we were young our parents were the world and their anxieties and pain mark our memory. The mark endures forever, it would seem, providing energy for the tight fist.

The infant child clings fiercely to its mother, for the comfort of the breast is supreme. Let go of that also? Letting go of the world is all right, when you fall to sleep in comforting arms. But let go of those arms? Let go so they can hold another? Let go to leave for school? Let go when death commands? Not easily, not willingly, not while strength lasts.

Control of time feels so urgent. Let go? Letting go allows the wheel of life to turn and gather speed, permitting change and loss, permitting death. We feel that world swirl by when our grip opens, when we surrender to the flow of change.

All things remind us of the possibility of change. Holding on to what has passed, inevitably we turn to face behind us, witnessing departures. Yet letting go permits our turning forward, into the flow of new arrivals, the stream of gifts from the unknown. Facing backward, how can we receive?

Males are taught that letting go is weak and passive. Passivity is female, so the lesson goes; it is the female who receives and pays with sexual submission. Letting go of feeling means "hysterical" and letting go too far will mean "insane." So we don't let go.

Finally, if letting go takes place, if the receptive mode prevails, the sharp boundary of the personal "I" may blur and dissolve, arousing panic at the emergence of an alien world.

Thus, the fist stays clenched despite a thousand exhortations to "let go."

One day an atheist was walking along a cliff when he slipped and fell over the edge. As he plunged downward, he managed to grab the branch of a small tree that was growing from a crevice in the rock. Hanging there, swaying in the cold wind, he realized how hopeless his position was. Far below were jagged boulders, and there was no way to climb up. His grip on the branch was weakening.

"Well," he thought, "only God can save me now. I've never believed in God, but I might be wrong. What have I to lose?"

So he called out, "God! If you exist, save me—and I'll believe in you!"

There was no answer. He called again.

"Please, God, I never believed in you, but if you'll save me now, I'll believe in you from now on."

Suddenly, a great voice boomed down from the clouds, "Oh, no you won't. I know your kind."

The man was so surprised he almost lost his grip on the branch.

"Please, God, you're wrong, I really mean it, I'll believe!"

"Oh, no you won't. That's what they all say."

The man pleaded and argued.

Finally, God said, "All right, I'll save you. Let go of the branch."

"Let go of the branch!" the man exclaimed. "Do you think I'm crazy?"

9.

Psychotherapy

So before you head East you may need a Western school, to relax your hand and help you out the door of your childhood's home. The first-level schools won't do; they are for information and tools for the object world: reading, writing, arithmetic, history, science, math. Even "literature" won't do the job. Art, music, and dance are taught as extras. When the budget gets cut, guess what goes? Only "English" survives, in the interest of our common culture, of being "well read." *Silas Marner,* served in treacle, puts the class to sleep. Our public schools are for the object world, the action mode, the realms of "me," "it," "mine"—and Time. They give you power over objects. They won't help with what you need now.

A second-level school is needed, to learn what you have never tried to know: the process of your thought, the way you lie and hide, and what is hidden—the secret workings of your fantasies, the forms of your fears. Our science helps us here, with information on development and psychological defense. We have a second-level school, born of that science which has become an art: psychotherapy. It doesn't go as far as Eastern schools, the eye of "I" is not examined, and after Body and Mind, the catalogue is blank. But it's a second-level school: Dependency and Letting Go are studied there. Perhaps you should enroll and take a course or two, in preparation.

Annoyed at the idea? Disappointed? In a hurry for a saffron robe? Be reassured: psychotherapy embodies Western wisdom, but its school has rules so close to Eastern thought you hear Freud in the Vedas: "The truth of Atman is revealed when a qualified aspirant, instructed by an illumined teacher, practices the disciplines of self-control, meditation, and inwardness of mind."

Let us examine this prescription and see what it can show us about this second-level school of the West, what it does and where it meets the East.

"The Truth of Atman." "Who are you? What are you?" These questions return again and again. Their answer is the enlightenment sought through spiritual paths. It is the justifying goal of a bewildering number of techniques and procedures that have been used as far back as we have history. Is there a different goal for Western science? Not really. The physicist and the biologist go deep into life to know what life is and what we are.

Atman, the True Self, is obscured by ignorance, the Vedas say, by misinterpretation of the sensory world, by conditioning of false assumptions that support the culture but imprison the man. The path of Freud also seeks "The Truth of Atman," the nature of the real self, and, for all its deficiencies, it has more explanations than the Vedas do for "ignorance." It talks of demons, too, of grotesque figures, the demons of fear, guarding the treasure of real knowledge. Illusion, too, is the foe of psychoanalysis, creating the illness of isolation. Self-inflicted blindness, said Freud, creates its own world, producing "transference" and the paranoid view. The psychotherapist knows that fear of what's inside, and fear of the body's death, creates a special world for reassurance. Sufism knows it, too:

ALL YOU NEED

"I'll have you hanged," said a cruel and ignorant king, who had heard of Nasrudin's powers, "if you don't prove that you are a mystic."

"I see strange things," said Nasrudin at once; "a golden bird in the sky, and demons under the earth."

"How can you see through solid objects? How can you see far into the sky?"

"Fear is all you need."   [Shah.]

The activity of Western psychotherapy holds up a mirror to the patient's mind, showing him his mental life. In the process, he dis-identifies. You cannot be your emotion when you look at it, when you examine its flavor and notice its beginning and its end. Something happens when you observe, when you join the therapist in watching, in noticing, with moral judgment set aside and replaced by interest and by awe at the creative madness of the fearful mind. Ramana Maharshi prescribed observing until the "I" was there and everything else was gone. Zen hammers at the "I"; Hasidism, too. Observation is a strong solvent; it dissolves identity. "Who are you?" Look and see. If my name changes, am I gone? Am I "psychiatrist," "American," "male," "tall"? The object words come thick, fast-flying through the air, like someone throwing rubber balls at a Plexiglas screen in front of you, who are watching. Lying on the analytic couch or sitting in the "hot seat," Gestalt style, the objective is the same: discovering a pattern that you didn't know you thought was you. "The Truth of Atman is revealed . . ." only under certain conditions.

"An Illumined Teacher." East or West, you must have a guide, someone who knows the way, the way to freedom, back through the eye. The therapist should have traveled the path before you, for he cannot show you what he himself has never seen. He must have reached a treasure on the road and, knowing it is there, persist until the patient finds it too.

He must be acquainted with demons, knowing how they're pumped and stuffed with air, seeing how it's done—inflation and deflation both. It's an "illumination" of a sort. When the patient's demon jumps out from behind a tree, making horrifying sounds, the therapist should be less afraid than the patient-child.

The therapist, too, must practice self-control, to avoid feeding the patient to the therapist's own demons. Abstinence is the therapeutic rule for both. Not chastity, but abstaining from gratifying the demons: the need to teach, to cure, to save (perhaps the most dangerous of all). Abstinence from being Daddy, from feeding a gaping mouth.

Someone said to Bahaudin Naqshband:
"You relate stories, but you do not tell us how to understand them."
He said:

"How would you like it if the man from whom you bought fruit consumed it before your eyes, leaving you only the skin?"   [Shah.]

Neither may the therapist protect himself; he must be free to act, not blocked by considerations of self-esteem or fear. He must stay open so that understanding can expand, so that he can be a channel producing the "good hour" when everything flows, when he acts without acting, when a process contains and extends him at the same time.

The therapist can see what the patient cannot—the free person shining, like a flower seen through weeds.

"*Qualified Aspirant.*" What qualifies you? "Sincerity," say the spiritual guides; "Motivation" say the psychiatric texts. Sincerity—wanting to know in order to be free. Motivation— the wish to know, stronger than fear.

In psychotherapy a war is fought with Fear. When you are a patient you find that all is smooth until the armies meet, then comes the chaos. A traitor schemes within, in league with the old life, advising flight no matter what the cost: "I think I've got as much out of this as I can at the moment, I'm thinking of stopping after this week." "You can't help me any- more, I need a different kind of treatment." Or—silence. Then, you don't return. You get close to something so important your mind tries to run away.

The problem is not new: "When you feel least interested in following the Way which you have entered, this may be the time when it is most appropriate for you. . . . You will always have doubts, but only discover them at a useful time for your weakness to point them out." (Shah.)

Courage, trust, humility—priceless qualities in searching for Atman, on the couch or off of it. Who is qualified? In ancient times, you sat seven days before the monastery gates. Psychotherapy should test more; money and time are not enough as indicators of sincerity.

"*Self-Control.*" The patient must not run. When monsters and witches rise from darkness, he must stand his ground in order to observe. No action prompted by anxiety can rule his mind. The gratification of dependency must be relinquished, as difficult to do as unclenching sticky fingers from around a lollipop. There should be no commotion, no noise. Only in stillness can one observe, like the stillness in the eye of a hurricane.

"Just sit," the Zen master instructs. "And then what?" asks the eager student. "Just sit" is the reply.

"*Meditation.*" Just sit, become the Witness, or call it "free association." Let go interpretation, analysis by intellect; allow the stream to be itself and watch. "There is my fear (I am not that)." "There is my desire (I am not that)." "There is my concept (I am not that)." Stillness, watching—meditation. Not different for the therapist. His action is to still the clamor of his ego and in that stillness allow intuition to be heard. "Free-floating attention" prescribe the psychoanalytic texts.

"Just sit!"

In psychotherapy, patient and therapist together watch the mental stream flow by. They learn dis-identification. They are so intent, so busy, they don't turn and glance ahead along the road they are traveling. The road leads to two mirrors standing face to face; it leads to a stunning fall into infinite space, shattering theories and pretensions. At ease in Objectland, unaware, therapist and patient dance along an exit to another world. "The patient learns to identify with the observing ego of the analyst." The observing ego, you say? Show it to us. ("Show me your true self," the Zen master cackles gleefully. "Who is it that has the thought?" asks the saintly yogi, cackling inside.) Pursue the "observing ego" and it steps behind you, out of sight and out of reach. No object can you find. Chase it madly, hunt it with the intellect, try to catch it with your rational mind—your sanity wavers, the Fiftieth Gate yawns wide. My mind fails, too. I cannot tell you what I do not know, and those who know cannot speak of it with words. The action mode is helpless here. Our minds can only show us that our minds have failed.

"What can I do?"

Be still, watch, listen.

The information of the second-level school will not be heard unless the eyes and ears are open, and they are closed for a reason. Resistance and defense, the illumination of Freud, requires a "journey" to the hidden jewel. One by one, resistances must fall apart, each lollipop dropping away until the hand is fully open to receive a different food. If you read the lives of the yogis, the Zen masters, the Sufis, and the Hasids, there comes Satori, Enlightenment—followed by more years of work, more meditation, and the everyday life. It is not Saturday night but Monday morning that is the time of journeying. Stage by stage, level by level, understanding must penetrate like water soaking steadily through a packed, dry soil. It's an inward journey, and meditation is an attitude.

There is no sudden transformation, all in a moment. Growth needs time.

"*Inwardness of Mind.*" The patient journeys inward to find his true self. Inward into the ego, into the "I," to understand how he has made his world, his demons, his gods, his form of perception. The therapist is inward too, listening to his inner life to tell him what he cannot see. Intuition, the voice from inside, becomes refined, but he must listen to his emotions too—all inner promptings showing the patient and the therapist in one continuous stream.

In ordinary life the intellect sits like a lid, covering and containing the interior force, the nutrition of change. After all, that's its job, to keep a focus on the outer world. Preoccupation with the self and inward journeys will not secure food. It is with outward energy that we master the biological world. Our intellects are tools for a certain function, marvelous in use, but it's hard to use a hammer to clean your hands; so all the disciplines say, "Put it down—for now." When the patient journeys inward, he sets the intellect aside, decommissioned, as it were, until a later time. Techniques can help: deep breathing, relaxation, free association, and imagery are used in East and West. Psychosynthesis, Gestalt, Reichian are therapies built on a bypass, routes that skirt the intellect, providing access to the interior.

The inward journey is a journey because the path is long. The intellect does not resign. What once was servant now rules the house and must be gradually restrained until, once again, it serves our needs, and those only. So we travel inward to freedom, inward until, perhaps, inward and outward are the same. "Where id was, there shall ego be," said Freud. Ego may be a bad translation. The word Freud used in German was "ich"—the "I".

Psychotherapy School and Spiritual School—Congruent Principles:

1. The truth will set you free, so understand yourself.

2. Increase the scope of your awareness, ("Where id was, there shall ego be.")

3. Confront your demons. Learn thereby they are your own creations, at your command.

4. Free yourself from attachments to the past (assumptions, conditioning) and from desire for the past (transference).

5. There is nothing to be afraid of.

6. You create your world; therefore there is hope and responsibility.

7. Flow with the flow, for you are alive and the organic is formed by interaction, as well as by design.

When the sufferer is the agent of his suffering, the doctor has a different role. Someday all body ills may fall under the same dynamic and there will be no division in the healing arts. Now it is psychotherapy that sees the villain and the victim in the same person and, therefore, does not "cure." The therapist points to the Self, the Other, the World, bringing them into the light of awareness. He and the patient hunt the origins of those ideas, hunt the motives, forces, energies maintaining them, feeding the "illness" that is the patient's creative work, his master plan. Those forces, fear, love, and guilt, must be examined so the door of the cage in the dark basement can be opened wide. Out of that gloom there staggers forward to greet us a small child, fearful, loving, bewildered. Psychotherapy can be a hand leading the child, who then finds the hand (his own) that leads him to sunlight.

There is something else that happens that cannot be defined: a transfer, a conduction of something good, of something healing, of something for which the therapist is source and channel both. Not to be measured or defined, it is there, felt over time, experienced beneath awareness, like air to us, water to the fish.

Psychotherapy school and spiritual school part company along the way. The teacher/therapist cannot teach what he does not know. The teacher/therapist will not see in the patient what he cannot see in himself and in the world.

The psychotherapist is limited in what he sees and knows. He may trust reason and intellect to define the world, and intellect does not go far enough. It must be left behind at some point to open the door for a different kind of knowing.

THE FIFTIETH GATE

Without telling his teacher anything of what he was doing, a disciple of Rabbi Barukh's had inquired into the nature of God, and in his thinking had penetrated further and further until he was tangled in doubts, and what had been certain up to this time became uncertain. When Rabbi Barukh noticed that the young man no longer came to him as usual, he went to the city where he lived, entered his room unexpectedly, and said to him: "I know what is hidden in your heart. You have passed through the fifty gates of reason. You begin with a question and think, and think up an answer—and the first gate opens, and to a new question! And again you plumb it, find the solution, fling open the second gate—and look into a new question. On and on like this, deeper and deeper, until you have forced open the fiftieth gate. There you stare at a question whose answer no man has ever found, for if there were one who knew it, there would no longer be freedom of choice. But if you dare to probe still further, you plunge into the abyss."

"So I should go back all the way, to the very beginning?" cried the disciple.

"If you turn, you will not be going back," said Rabbi Barukh. "You will be standing beyond the last gate: you will stand in faith." [Buber.]

Ordinary reason cannot be trusted to carry you all the way. Nor can ordinary emotion do the job. Such feelings cannot be used to plumb the world; they are mixed and rooted in a world gone by: the past.

Most important of all, psychotherapists stand on a plain whose basic dimension is the separate self. Discontent arises from that separate self, but the solution cannot be found because the ground of the self on which the therapist stands is not open to challenge—he does not see it, it is too close and too big. The universe viewed from that Western stance is mechanical and meaningless, for it is based on abstractions and abstractions are empty. Meaning is not a product of language, or object logic, of the action mode. Meaning is *experienced* and therefore outside the mode and outside our science.

Finally, at some point the patient must go alone. What he

needs to learn by his experience cannot take place in dependency on the therapist, on a guru, or on God. Psychoanalytic theory was brave, indeed. By design it plotted to give back parental power to the patient, to analyze the "transference" until the power that was projected was reclaimed. No other Western institution has this goal, not government, not church, not school; but practice differs from the theory. Therapists, and spiritual teachers, too, may fail in that transfer, and the patient/student stays behind. Dependency systems are all the same; they cannot pass you through the door. No matter how grand the vistas they survey, the view is from the doorway of the living room, and the living room, exotic and brilliant though it may be, is still the child's home.

10.

Third-Level School

Psychotherapy school is a school for the lower grades, a prep school for the next stage: the third-level school that teaches What You Are. Its curriculum, "death" of the "self" and awakening of "intuition," is taught by no school that you would recognize. It, too, begins with unlearning.

Unlearning the Self

The strangest part of this strange world is yourself. There are so many varieties of you, moment by moment, state by state, that only a very selective memory allows the illusion of a constant, continuous self to be maintained.

Think about all the various conditions that constitute your life. Sometimes you are in a state of remembering and ninety per cent of you is—at that moment—memories. Sometimes you are emotional, angry or ecstatic or sad, and ninety per cent of what is you is that emotion. At other times you may be what you see, or what you fantasize. Sometimes it's a mixture, fifty-fifty; it really doesn't matter.

Through all these variations, all these changes, you assume that you are there. Indeed, sometimes "I am" may be your only feeling, very powerful, very "spacey." Most of the time, you're too busy, so it's ninety per cent of something else.

You have so many selves: the thought self, the body self, the I-am self, the I-want self, the emotion self; perhaps the left-brain self, the right-brain self, the limbic self, and the mid-brain self. So many, so changing, not continuous at all. Each self appears and disappears, fades from view while another takes its place. So where in all this are you? If you are your experience and that experience always changes, what makes you think you have a self at all?

What of the times when the "I" is zero, when you are engrossed in a movie or performing some action too quickly to permit thought? You assume, nevertheless, that you have been there all along. That "I" is discontinuous, but your memory fills in the gaps, just as your eyes create an optical illusion by filling in the "correct" line.

"What's the difference?" you may ask. "Other people are witness that I don't disappear." You are right. But the "I" they see and the "I" you mean may not be the same.

When you began, aged zero, you did not assume that "you" were there or that anyone else was there when he had passed from sight. "Out of sight, out of mind," and out of thought, as well. Maturation enabled you to find the pea under the shell of memory. Once you remembered, you could predict, and soon your existence needed no proof—because existence itself had changed. Where once it had been all sensation, now thought and memory had become real, most real of all.

"Mine, me, you, and I, in that order." In that order we create ourselves. Emotions become "mine." Thoughts are "mine"; whose else could they be? Desires are mine; what is more me than my wants? And fear is "mine," for who else will die? Mine becomes "me," the social object, collector of labels, possessor of things. "Me" encounters "you," the object, the Other, who tells us we are objects, too, and tricks us into categories that enclose us like snug beds: man, woman, Indian chief.

"I think, therefore I am."

No, you are not your thoughts. Your thinking tells you that you exist. The structure of your sentences implies an "I." The logic of your thought points to a subject, even when the subject isn't there to see. Have you ever looked at a picture that illustrates "perspective"? Dotted lines emerge from houses and from trees, marching to a focus straight off the page, aimed at you, the viewer. The picture says you're there: "All these objects point to you—so you're an object, too!" The linear perspective in our thoughts converges backward to an empty space. So you fill it in. And color it.

What do you color the object you? Color it with more thinking, with emotion, with desires, and with fear. Use all the "inside" colors to make it bright and clear.

"What about emotions? They, at least, are mine!"

Emotions are signals for response of body and of mind. They program the physiological circuits for the pre-set plan. Sadness, for example, slows us down, "depresses" us. Our depressions follow loss; the loss of mother meant the threat of death for the child. It had to wait for the mother's return or for a substitute. Depression serves a purpose: to conserve life. This theory is confirmed by research with infant monkeys, separated from their mothers. First they are active, searching and crying. Then they huddle, nonmoving, "apathetic," and withdrawn. The heart rate slows, the metabolic rate falls; conserving its reserves, the organism waits. Efficiently, it meets the threat.

Anger mobilizes for defense, not against abandonment but against attack. The heart rate quickens, breathing is fast, and vision narrows to the threat. The strategy is counterattack. The emotional signal, like Paul Revere, storms through the physiological streets, wakening the citizens to armed action.

Joy releases tension. It halts stress responses and remotivates the organism for creative life. Joy kills fear and catapults you outward to embrace the world.

"What about love?"

Love opens you, decreasing barriers to union, relaxing muscles, eyes, and mind, and permitting a flow of energy outward and inward for nurturing of growth and creation. Yet there are different kinds of "love," perhaps for the different functions of mother, lover, teacher—and different systems, too: self, species, life. As the function varies, the means will vary, too, requiring many kinds of love, some not emotional at all.

Fear tells you you are there. When all else fails, fear will rise in panic to sound alarm at the approaching end of the object self. So loyal in your defense, so faithful, watchful, at your side—you trust him most of all. Yet, he's corrupt. Without you as object, fear must go. He shrieks: "Look out! Don't listen! It's a trick!" His job's at stake. Without an object self, what cause for fear? Fear protects itself.

We do not realize with what efficiency we function. For instance, we feel sad and do not know its purpose. And it's more complicated now. Our emotions have been elaborated and woven into a symbolic world. Threats of abandonment or attack can now be more abstract than a monkey can conceive. Our rage can turn within, killing us; our grief can slow us down to a dull coma, conserving energy against the return of a lost bank account we do not need. "Love" can short-circuit, turning our energy back to us, never passing beyond our mental skin. Yet the roots are the same: functional signals. Ignorantly, we bow to our emotions in mindless awe because they are so "personal." Yet, we are not them. Emotions serve us, or should.

"What about desire? I want, therefore I am."

When you want two things at once—in conflict—is that you? Or do your urges answer to biological needs, to patterns in the genes and to lessons learned at home, buttons in the psyche that anyone can push behind the scenes: "Don't take that lying down!" "He stole my idea"; "Her blouse is unbuttoned, I can see . . ."; "It's transformed my life, do you want some, too?" "She snubbed me"; "I climb a mountain because it's there"; "All you can eat!"

Possessing gives life to the object self, to the Thing. "I want," the energy of possession; "I have," the locus of possession, of substance, of mortality; "I will," the energy of intention put to work collecting; and, then there is "me," the social object, staggering forward with all my attributes in a huge bundle on my back, like a peddler.

Possession creates suffering, and pain hurts because it's "mine." Pain, old buddy, what happens when I step a pace away, look you squarely in the eye, inspect you head to toe like a new recruit? "What's your shape, mister? What color are you? Hot or cold? Thick or thin?" Pain—old buddy—you begin to change, learn manners, drop your eyes, turn in your badge of power.

Behind pain, in a line, stand all the others: vision, hearing, all the senses—a whole company of pseudoselves. After inspection, they're more obedient to your command.

There is no end to object-making. Go to India, climb the highest mountain, and sit cross-legged observing all the other objects, all the inside colors, until you become, finally, the Witness, the finest object of them all.

"Then the next stage is concentration upon the idea of limitless consciousness. Here one does not dwell on limitless space alone, but one also dwells upon the intelligence which perceives the limitless space as well. So ego watches limitless space and consciousness from its central headquarters. The empire of ego is completely extended, even the central authority cannot imagine how far its territory extends. Ego becomes a huge, gigantic beast." (Trungpa.)

Most of us are content with the usual "I's": young, old, handsome, dumb . . . and on and on. What a collection! Look at all we think is part of us: joy, anger, calculations, desires, objects, labels, fear, and "soul." Look at that merry-go-round, the way it spins, and then, watching it go round, perhaps suddenly you'll ask, "How do I know it's me?" The question seems absurd and never does get asked aloud. For we have entered Objectland. We have become a Thing and reap our reward: identity with all the Others, the reassurance of our kind. We need that reassurance now that we are objects.

The Velvet Crowbar

Spiritual school goes beyond psychotherapy school when it teaches the unlearning of these selves. The self of thought, the self of emotion, the self of desire, the self of sensation—all must be unlearned. These conditioned selves cling to you as shells and vegetation cling to a tide-washed rock. But the schools know what to do; they have many ways to clean the stone. Meditation is a velvet crowbar that pries thought-mussels loose, leaving the bare surface to be bathed again by the sea. The crowbar slides beneath emotions, too; those clumps of feeling, those subtle forms of memory, open and close like the carnivorous flowers they are, all mouth and color—now separate from the rock, afloat in the wash of the tide. In school, in meditation, sitting like a rock, just sitting, you let sensations spatter like the spray and drip away, polishing the rock until it reflects back the sun.

Desires are the last to loosen. They are lodged like petrifications in the heart and must dissolve away. Many things are tried: the ascetic life; koan dynamite; the hypnotic energy of dance and the deep chant, resonating in the center; the teaching story, holding a mirror to the form of desire; and, finally, the Teacher, whose radiant vibration shakes the atoms of the stone into harmony and peace and praise in the rhythm of the sea.

The mirror of the School shows you many selves, shifting, changing: the I of intention, the I of I am, the I of emotions, the I of possession, the I of the body, and the I described by Others. These selves have functions; you need to use them all for living in the world. Unlearning is a step to freer use. But you cannot use what is weak or hidden. Our Western culture, like an obsessive tailor, has spent so much time on the intellect-jacket, it has yet to get around to the emotion-shirt and the body-pants. No wonder we are a spectacle, displaying our new clothes, annoyed at the laughter of children, yet haughty. Not long ago, some new tailors set up shop in California, where East meets West. Now, there are so many tailors they don't know whose needle they are using, but, back then, the Esalen shop opened a new frontier: fitting the shirt and pants. The emotional self and the body self were taught in class. Encounter by the sea, massage and sex, here-and-now orgasms for "intimate strangers." How ridiculous! The New York tailors almost died from laughter but were saved by indignation at the sight of so many customers discarding jackets in California. The colors of the shirts were often weird and the pants let it all hang out, but at least they were clothes that gave warmth to the heart and to all that land below the waist. Although Wilhelm Reich, a tailor of the body self, died in prison (he opened up his shop too soon), times have changed, the body has returned, although it still is seen as an appendage to the head.

Esalen is more than laughs; how strange to find one's state of mind sparkle like a fresh-rinsed glass when it receives a body bath. The emotion self emerging from a Weekend smiles with delight to see the sky again. Strange how the wrinkles disappear and the face is young, how the thinking slows and senses sharpen when the rediscovery is made. Catharsis and the body, old-fashioned clothes, indeed, to be selling so briskly—but that's the Frontier West, you know, no sophistication, no culture, no tradition.

Yes, the body has returned, bringing with it sensual life and feeling. Just in time. The spiritual schools teach letting go of self—but not to babies, or adolescents, or psychic cripples, deformed beyond belief. The Western student knocking at the door presents a gigantic inflated head, spindly legs, and a sunken chest, and announces with intellectual fervor, "I surrender!" What a prize! There cannot be a harvest before the crop is grown. Before the self is ripe, what can you dare to give away? When the conceptual self disappears, when the head is gone, the intellectual has little left. "It's Death!" shrieks the swollen head, watching itself vanish in the mirror of the School. "It's Death!" it cries, and flees or goes hysterical. Without the body self, without knowing you are there, in your breath, in your belly, in your thighs and chest, what will rescue you from panic when "you" "disappear"?

No wonder the Schools have strange routines, depending on the students who stumble to the door. Weird diets, heavy work, incense, singing, meditation, dancing, breathing, postures, flowers, swords, or sex may be prescribed. Five or seven chakras, say the texts, form the path and source of energy that needs to flow without constriction. So open all the chakras, one by one. Until you are fully there, in all your strength, you do not have the power to surrender.

The many routines work, but for whom are they correct? The druggist lines his shelves with little bottles; a doctor must prescribe. Which medication is right for you? Maybe none. Go to a doctor, if you can find one. The diagnosis should be made before the treatment starts and you've been ill a long time. Leave the drugstore, you don't know what the labels mean and it isn't candy on the shelves, despite the bright colors. Go find a doctor (teacher). Now.

"Where?"

"Try the Yellow Pages: 'If you are really sincere, you will find a teacher.' 'The door is always open.' 'You are already in the Teacher's hands.' "

The Teacher

So you look around and find there are so many teachers of so many things; the first problem confronting you is to choose. The advertising is unrestrained. No FCC to limit claims; each one says it will take you there, to bliss, to peace and kundalini. Enlightenment is in the bag; just follow the guru, roshi, rinpoche, pir, baba, buba, reb, swami, reverend, or hippie saint, clothed in white, yellow, blue, orange, red or brown. Take your pick. That's the problem. How do you know if this or that one is for you?

Let us imagine that you see a poster: "Teacher is in town!" You go to hear him. He's younger than you'd thought or wanted. It bothers you. You say so. This is his reply:

"What you're really asking is whether I have the Big

Truth. If I had a long white beard you'd think it more likely. You want me to have it in my pocket; then all you have to do is kiss my feet, be a good boy, be a good girl, and I'll finally pat you on your nice little head and give you your reward: Enlightenment! You're afraid I'm not old enough to have it in my pocket, that's your problem. You're a conniver who's looking for an angle you can play and so you come to me—the mark—to rip me off in perfect sanctity with your eyes rolled up to Heaven, counting your beads and muttering your mantra. How does it go? 'Lord Jesus, Krishna, Allah-kazam, seven-come-eleven for the promised land.' Well, it won't work, and if I fell for that baloney I'd be a bigger fool than you and all the others like you, with your flattery and coyness and preening and tears and awe and all that damn emotion."

He leans forward. "What do you want? Do you know? Do you want me to take care of you? Well, I won't, it doesn't interest me, I have childern of my own. So that's out. Do you want Enlightenment? Why do you want that when you don't even know what it is? What do you think will happen when you get it? Answer me!"

You manage to reply, "I don't want to be afraid of Death and I want to be content and happy—like the time I had a mystical experience. The books say you can be that way all the time, once you're Enlightened."

He groans in mock pain. "My God! Didn't it occur to you that solving your problems comes *first!?* When you examine all your problems and see what's going on, when you figure out why you're scared of dying, when you start being happy, and when you cut out all this crap, then, perhaps, a Teacher might have something to show you—if you still needed anyone to show it to you."

"Then what's a Teacher for?"

"To get you to work on yourself—the last thing you want to do, because you're lazy or you think it's hopeless or it will take too long."

"But I do need help, even for that; and what if I make a mistake and choose you when you're not the right one or I don't choose you and it turns out you're the one I need—then I've blown my chance and it will be too late!"

"You'll miss the Good Ship Lollipop! Too bad! There it goes, your last chance, sailing away toward the bright horizon, leaving you unhappy and forever alone on the cold shore. Now there's a fantasy to keep you scrambling like a beetle for your whole life!"

He pauses, thinks, then continues, slower: "Look, it's not finding some Big Truth that's the issue, but your growth. You are like a plant in the ground that is growing: if you are three inches high with three leaves poking up out of the ground, you are not going to be an oak tree three months from now. Indeed, the attempt to be an oak tree would destroy you. You must grow from where you are. Furthermore, you may really be some other kind of tree. We need more than oak trees in this world, you have to allow your own growth to take place.

"For instance, if what I'm saying is helpful, then you are using me as a Teacher. If what I am saying is not helpful, then you are not able to. No big deal! No tragedy! We both are doing what we can. All you can do, and all you will do, is to learn what you are ready to learn. And all that takes is an interest in learning, in watching, in seeing, in trying to understand your own nature. The activity is life-long and interesting. In its own way, it's a delight.

"We are in the position of looking around from where we are standing to those areas we do not understand, that are still unknown. That's the position of all of us; and that position provides freshness and the joy of discovering the new, the yet unseen, the yet uncontrolled, that which is the *aliveness* of growth.

"Don't be afraid that you will fail, that you will make a mistake and not guess under which cup the pea is hidden. There is no pea for you to find. There is only the process of becoming more sane, more real, truly alive. If you look, you will see exactly what your eyes are able to see and use at that time, and if you can have some trust in that process, you will enjoy your life and growth and be free from the fear that holds you where you are now.

"So you see, there is nothing to be afraid of, and there is nothing to lose. There is only the experience of learning, of freedom, of interest and wonder at the vast reality, beyond anything you have seen, to which you belong."

11.

The Path as a Multistage Rocket: A Speculation

You enter your path of learning before you are born. By just being, you begin—for the first stage of your journey is pure experience—the self of happening, the unknowing experience of the maternal flux. No adjectives we now use will fit, for words need memory to provide comparison.

Gradually, the happenings of pressure, movement, and vibration come into focus, increase in depth and shape as discrimination grows. But, still, you are not there. Reality glows with consciousness, yet unselfconscious still. The stress of birth, and later shocks, stimulates intention—a direction for energy and the birth of a new happening: action. The organism moves, in purposeful response to the urgings that are triggered by discomfort and threats to life. Action spells the end of the pre-self world. The action mode, as it selects and shapes a world, selects and shapes a self—you are born a second time. Danger, pain, and desire release energy, and the body grows, and the world grows with it. The personal self is shaped like soft clay, then fired in the kiln of social life until it hardens; it can be changed a little, here and there, with pressure, but the basic form remains.

Everyone goes thus far along the path. From happening to action to self—we go that far, seeking to expand, but the clay shell of the self does not yield and we feel trapped. Dissatisfaction in a hundred forms erupts like weeds, converting the world's garden into a ruin. Yet dissatisfaction is our energy, too, and if its pressure has strength and the shell of the self is not too thick, cracks appear through which we catch a glimpse of light, tantalizing and remote. Psychotherapy can thin the shell and widen the cracks if it treats dissatisfaction as an ally, as a live force pounding on the door asking for health. The Teachers of the spiritual schools stand on the other side, in the light of the space beyond self. They can tell you there is freedom, they may even reach a hand that you can grasp to help step through; but no one takes that step, save you, and at the self's threshold there may be no light that you can see. You have just an urging from within, as you struggle with fear.

We may travel a long time approaching the threshold. Our path is like a type of rocket-to-the-moon, with several stages. At birth the earliest desire was set in motion, an urge for freedom from an enclosing form. An archetype of evolution, it sets the course for freedom. In the same birth is born control, the urge to master the changing world, preventing the return to chaos. So we grasp the world to take command, striving to achieve control, to travel at a comfortable pace to a destination we select. Struggling with objects, we become an object, gathering the power we will need to make our journey.

With intellect, with skill, with culture, with science, and with the time won from biological needs, we build a ship for traveling upward—through space—to the destination plotted in our bones. The journey's end is unseen, but it draws us from within.

Stage One, the stage of self, may take a lot of time developing the thrust that sets you free from gravity, from the earth's pull. The action mode has built a great engine, the object self, and dissatisfaction is the fuel. It finally sets the ship in motion, blasting off the pad with great commotion. And off you go, gathering speed, nosing through the clouds and heading for your rendezvous with a "spiritual" school, a way station in space, orbiting our world, between the earth and the stars. It may look different from what you thought. The pictures of the old Schools do not help in recognizing the new; their forms change to suit the times. But if your fuel lasts and your engine doesn't falter and your radar stays true, you make your rendezvous, connecting with a Teacher and a School.

Then the work begins in preparation for your further flight. That work requires energy, too; and at first you use dependency for fuel. The wish for parents shifts to guru or to god (mother and father can take many forms). In the beginning you are delighted and encouraged by what you find, doing all those "spiritual" things. Blissful sensations abound. Time and space alter, as you do what you are told, and the self rejoices at these victories. So much hope arises that joy and love come bubbling forth, and utter satisfaction permeates the room. As Time is shaken, Death is shaken, too. Aging loses terror and aloneness fades away. Enfolded in the presence of the Teacher, trust returns and the hands of Buddha-Jesus-guru rest lightly on your head. Your fantasies have come true, it seems. Reunion with the Parent is achieved—you think. "At last, I've come home!" And indeed you have. But that kind of home is not much different from the original, and so the joy doesn't last or is succeeded by despair. In the end, for most, it's blissful enough, for their energy of growth is not so strong and dissatisfaction subsides; the shell of the self may be so thick that the interior disturbance is contained and the voyager stops there. Everyone around may confirm what seems to be completion of the trip. Joyful eyes reflecting joyful eyes seem evidence enough. The "blissed-out" student-child, watching himself on the stage of his fantasy, sees himself dressed in all the traditional clothes. "I'm happy and carefree—like a Zen monk." "I'm ascetic and pure—like a yogi." "I'm full of love—like a Sufi saint." The energy of growth still hammers from inside the shell but is not noticed with all that song and dance going on outside.

The schools are smarter than you might think. They know that action and dependency will go only so far, and then a different kind of power must be used. Receptive energy begins to build behind the scenes. Communal living, meditation, chanting, dance, robes, texts, and lectures do their work: they undermine the action mode, teaching the receptive. The Teacher says "stop," "sit," "be," and, finally, you do what you are told—you quit for a moment or a while. Then: more bliss! More joy! "I've got it! I'm enlightened! Wait until I tell my friends!" But, still, it doesn't last and if you're lucky, your eyes won't stay crossed in bliss. When it goes away, a new hunger will be born: you want it back, you want more. You want to make it permanent, that brief experience of "grace," "enlightenment," "peace." "Fine," says the Teacher, "just keep on sitting, dancing, working, reading . . . keep working! If you have any gaining idea in mind, however, that will ruin it; so just be aware of all your greed. And if you are afraid, that will block you, so don't run away; experience the fear. If you have pride, however, the spell won't work, so taste your vanity and spit it out." Under such scrutiny the object self shrivels, little by little. Greed is turned against itself.

"Teacher, I try and try, it works for a while and then I'm back again where I began. It's no use!"

"Then give it up! Cease your striving; just sit, just be, just do; allow, receive."

Exhausted, you let go, you stop, and something else begins to move. Nonstriving energy now begins to work, receptive power lifting you above the school, away from structures of the object self, into the space Beyond Self. The fantasies of dependency and possession that have led you to the school have been used, if you are lucky, to upset your plans. The lure of dependent dreams has led you to a destination you had not foreseen. Separation from Stage One has begun, using a new fuel, the power of surrender.

The hollow cylinder of Stage One that housed spiritual striving, the object self, dependency, and its defenses turns in empty space, and you watch it shrink, receding. It takes a long time to disappear from sight, but the distance widens as you gain speed.

What do you see beyond self? What can be said beyond

self? Words are from the object world and the syntax of our language is bound by its rules. Perhaps our rocket metaphor will carry us further, and speculation, while not itself the truth, can point the way or stir an awareness that needs no words.

We started with the self-as-happening and then became an object self. Mixed in were moments of the self-beyond, when attention, usually gathered around the object self, like iron filings at a magnet pole, was able to detach itself and cluster on the opposite pole—the world. When we detach from the object self, the world comes in, occupying the space that had been us. In our ordinary lives, the self-beyond is a momentary thing, but in that moment may be endless time, no-time, eternity.

Life is not fixed and nothing in reality stands still. Cessation of the object self is but a doorway, and on the other side is still a self, the self-beyond, an intangible locus from which the universe is seen. That locus is alive. The self-beyond is process, in a world of process that has no end and is not you and is not me. You see, my words are failing here, becoming mush. In this realm, paradox is king. You've heard the classic puzzles, the teasing insult, the slap at equilibrium, the lure: "Why did Bodhidharma come to China?" Answer: "An oak tree in the garden." Or: "Surrender to the guru until you learn the guru is yourself." Meaningless words to the object self but what more can be said? Beyond self unifies the doer, the doing, and what is done. (More word mush.) The unself-consciousness energy of the self-beyond moves mountains, does "miracles," and connects the stars and you. (Mystic mush.)

I see Stage Two spiraling upward above my head; it turns so fast and the light glancing from it is so dazzling that it blurs my sight, but I can see the outline of its form and see the connecting wires where they broke away. Higher and higher it goes until there is another sound (or is it a sound?), and then it disappears and cannot be seen at all from where I stand. Are there other stages? I don't know; it has become invisible. Has self disappeared into everything? I cannot see it any more, so I cannot say.

12.

Watching

It is not necessary to understand everything from where you are; just realize what sort of journey you are on. The realization eliminates despair and guides your energies. The trip should be enjoyed; don't be afraid. "There is no cause for fear. It is imagination, blocking you as a wooden bolt holds the door. Burn that bar. . . ." (Shah.) Enjoy the trip. When it's all over, you may wonder why you were in such a hurry, why you were looking so far ahead.

Meanwhile, the world is very real and there is so much to do. With some idea of the problem, we can begin to talk about solutions, something practical for John Doe, who is worried about the price of eggs and gasoline, who reads of terrorists with atomic bombs, who is asked for money to save the millions from starvation, and who cannot see the mountains because the smog has raised a gray-brown curtain, obscuring and poisoning his world. What's he to do with his dissatisfaction and his fear in a world that's spinning toward the grandest crisis of them all? John Doe-me, John Doe-you, there will be no Messiah; there is just you and the rest of us like you. What can we do? After all this talk of schools and mystics, selves and rockets, what's a realistic person supposed to do—now?

If you haven't found a Teacher and your job is nine to five, you may wonder what to do, how to begin to shake loose from the clay shell that sticks to you and makes it hard to breathe. There's a lot that you can do, plenty to keep you busy, and it turns out that you are the one who finally has to do the job. Start now, don't waste time. It's like a battle in the old days, hand-to-hand. Your enemy is strong, so unsheathe your sharpest sword, the one you have always carried but seldom used—watching.

You need to watch to see who's been in charge, because up to now you've been an automated slave. Part of your training is to think, "I'm free! I'm free!" while your robot circuits buzz and the gears click and your head bobs like a puppet.

There are buttons sticking out all over you waiting to be pushed. There's one called "Don't let him get away with it." Try the green one: "Selfish!" There's also, "Hurry up, you'll miss your . . ." How about, "You're wonderful!" or, "You understand, not like the rest." See the pink one? It says, "You're sexy—here's your chance!" There's a purple one, "You deserve it, don't listen to them," and a brown one, "Work hard, don't quit." The biggest button says, "What will they think of me?"

No, you're not free, but you can be. Begin by watching. Watch the things that seem to be most you: your feeling states. For example, try depression, if that's your style. Watch it rise so gray and foglike, so sad and soft and comforting. It's like an old pal, arm around your shoulder, leaning heavily on you in a narcotic embrace. Its gray fog blots out all disturbing details and leads you straight to bed and helplessness. What a relief! You've worked hard, and now, with all those savings of resentment and doubt, you can retire. Watch yourself become a child. Sink into bed. No effort is required; no effort is possible. Just suck your lollipop and wait till mama comes home. You've been deprived of what you need and are defective, and the world is a big bully. There's nothing to be done. Just watch the negative thoughts do their dance: "It's the same old thing"; "What's the use?" "I'll never make it"; "To hell with it"; "No one gives a shit"; and on and on. Watch them twirl in a ludicrous ballet. Watch—and walk away. You'll probably see depression trail behind, nagging for attention like an irritable child. Keep on walking—pat its head, understanding how it feels, but you're not going to go that way today. Don't try to throttle the rotten brat; just watch its antics with an interested eye. Compassion goes a long way.

What about falling in love? That's a feeling state, too. Should you watch that also? "I'm most gloriously me when I'm in love." Okay. But watch it; just watch the ecstasy while your eyes cross or bulge with delight at having found the one person who meets your needs—all of them. What a relief! To have found her/him after all that anxious waiting; now everything will be all right. Your delight assures you it is so. The excitement is so alive you vibrate with joy. Watch it. But don't start watching it until the merry-go-round has gone on long enough for you to tire of the thrill, and find out what falling in love is. When you've had enough, just watch—and step off, for that you will be able to do.

Watching is a powerful sword. It cuts through fantasies with one clean stroke, and feeling states, too, and the social reflex, and the thousand selves answering the buttons, saluting the commands.

Watch your usual self. Which self are you? You're a housewife. Fine! Which housewife on television are you? Or are you the housewife in a book you read, or are you just your mother? There's sure to be a picture flickering on the movie screen behind your eyes, telling you what to see and do and think as you play the role. It's Method Acting for everyone. You're a professional, although you didn't know it. Step back and watch the idiot perform—be interested, admire all your skill in being someone else. How well you learned! Admire all your friends—they do well, too; everyone's playing in their theater-in-the-round.

You're a bright young man. Fine! You know the part: you watched it, read it since you went to school. There you are, intent, setting all else aside, just like that guy in the movie you saw years ago, or yesterday. In the film, there's a wise old man who is watching you, looking out for you and passing you the power, 'cause he's the one who finally informs the world you're great, a Father who rewards his son—together you defy the Rest. (There's a Girl somewhere among the props.) You've a good role, you're something special with unlimited potential, and you'll never grow old, only up.

Or be the wise old man—now that's a part! Gentle, kind,

firm, and loved, while all admire your gray head and bend their knees in true submission. Pretty ones, too, when they're not screwing, will come to you with trust. Serene, above it all, you comfort them.

Or be the citizen: do your duty! Or the black man: defend your pride! Or the new woman: don't let the bastards put you down! Father, mother, sexpot, wife, he-man, real man, victim of life. The curtain is open, the audience never goes home—you're on! Every day, all the time. Watch your own show.

Once you watch it you're off the stage. So join the audience and you're almost there, another step will take you out the door.

"How do I know when I'm on stage?"

"By how you see."

There are some special kinds of vision when you're on a stage. I think you'll recognize them all:

Painter's vision. Your eyes sweep the scene like an artist's brush, splattering emotional paint on the canvas of your world. For example, when you do Justified Anger, you use a solid red with brown and purple flecks in an even wash that leaves the details clear, but with all perspective gone. Edge to edge, hostile power binds the canvas in dynamic unity. The painting's from a classical school, but prime examples can be found at every age. No first-rate collection is without one. Another kind of work is Spiritual Glow. This school of portraiture employs a shimmering golden blue; the brush strokes are pointillist, little dots of light radiate throughout. In the most intense examples of its kind, it creates a kind of glare.

The finest examples employ glow-behind-the-eyes and include some works in the best modern style. *I've Got a Secret* is typical. In this ingenious masterpiece, the letters of the title are formed from all the elements of smile and eyes and radiant concern that are the focus of this spiritual scene. The paint's a special blend, transparent yet opaque, so that you're never sure if what the artist is doing is revealing or concealing. If not done well, of course, a delightful ambiguity turns vulgar; spiritual paint requires the utmost taste.

Almost everyone can learn to use Depression paint. The cool gray tones create a monochrome whose power resides in the subtle variations of the depth of tone, a kind of visual smog that infiltrates the world so that the gray vision of the artist encloses the spectator without his even noticing. Everything dissolves in aching peace, somber, but, in its own way, brilliant!

Reverse vision. The eyeballs turn around and focus all perception inside the skull on fantasy and remembered dramas. You become engrossed in the scene inside. You're like a man sitting on a donkey, backward, convinced you're facing forward because the scene you see is in the direction that you are looking. It's dreaming out of bed and it has the quality of dreams: the details aren't really there, the scene is vague for all its vivid emotional charge. After you have watched it for a while, you may feel a strange sort of pain, a kind of subtle headache telling you you've been too long at the movies.

Limbo vision. This is the commonest sign of the actor. Not here, not there, you're somewhere in between. Your vision stops before it reaches the live reality of the face, the tree, the scene confronting you. Only outlines register upon your radar screen, enough to identify a friend or foe, to name, respond, and move away. Your focus hovers in the air, suspended between worlds—not here, not there—floating in between, receiving signals from both globes, but safely disconnected. You may not know you're out in space until you make the effort to connect, and as you draw closer to the ground the details of the world appear. With marvelous concreteness something live emerges and you can feel the energy come out to you, filling up your empty space; space, you realize now, that was horribly cold.

13.

Rebelling

It isn't enough to watch. At some point you must act, defiantly. You're like a city that's been enslaved so long you think the army camped outside is for your protection. Once you see what's going on, it's time to rebel. It will be a fight and you'll stand alone, for your most trusted men—your words and thoughts—are in the pay of the enemy. They must be overthrown, for it is they that keep you trapped within the city walls, creating a maze in which your energy is drained and you are led back to the same point from which you began.

Words and thoughts evolved to help us manage an overwhelming world. As an algebra for experience, we use them for rapid calculations and for building complicated plans to ensure survival in a savage world. Indeed, the biological world is a gaggle of mouths, one devouring the other until all are swallowed in turn. By abstracting from this world a code of language, we have become the largest mouth of all. The symbolic mouth, worked by hidden levers, does a fine job indeed; in fact, it's big enough now to swallow the world, but we have forgotten who it is that's working the levers. It's as if the Wizard of Oz had become so engrossed in the puppet head he made that he prayed to it for help and forgiveness.

For example, consider the white matter of the brain. Neurological books, heavy and full, contain precise descriptions of the "organ of the mind," the brain, and the white matter which is a part of it: "The white matter of the cerebral hemispheres is shown to best advantage in horizontal sections of the brain. . . . It is then seen as an apparently homogeneous mass filling all available spaces between the surface gray matter (cerebral cortex) and the subcortical gray matter (basal ganglia and thalamus)." (Didio.) The white matter is evidently "real." But let's imagine how its discovery was made. You be the surgeon and we'll look through your eyes, although the process may not sound like anything you have read—until now.

As you begin, you experience a field of sensations which you have learned by practice to see in stable patterns called "table" and "body." In the center of the field, you experience a familiar pattern that you symbol-name "a brain." Using sensations linked to the symbols "muscles" and "knife," you bring about a regulated change in patterns of visual sensations, a successive alteration in the "brain" configurations; you label that orderly change "cutting." Eventually, you experience a pattern of sensations not previously symbol-labeled and, therefore, "new." To this pattern of sensations you give the symbol name "white matter," and, characteristically, you automatically regard the pattern as more "real" than the actual process by which you discovered it, that process being labeled "mental."

The "brain" is derived from sensations and thought—not vice versa. Yet, haven't you been taught that the brain and body are "physical" and real, but your thoughts are "subjective"? Haven't you been taught that the world is more real than you?

Theoretical Physics: The Subversive Science

We are educated in precision. Ambiguity is the sin of science. It had been cast out, or so we thought, until we had to grapple with the ultralarge and the ultrasmall. Then, the more precise our scientific terms, the more error they led us to, for they were further from experience. The physicist Heisenberg writes:

> Furthermore, one of the most important features of the development and the analysis of modern physics is the experience that the concepts of natural language, vaguely defined as they are, seem to be more stable in the expansion of knowledge than the precise terms of scientific language, derived as an idealization from only limited groups of phenomena. This is in fact not surprising since the concepts of natural language are formed by the immediate connection with reality; they represent reality. It is true that they are not very well defined and may therefore all undergo changes in the course of the centuries, just as reality itself did, but they never lose the immediate connection with reality. On the other hand, the scientific concepts are idealizations; they are derived from experi-

ence obtained by refined experimental tools, and are precisely defined through axioms and definitions. . . . But through this process of idealization and precise definition, the immediate connection with reality is lost.

Heisenberg goes on to emphasize the fundamental stability of the concepts of natural language such as "mind," "the human soul," "life," and "God"; and he concludes, "We know that any understanding must be based finally on the natural language because it is only there that we can be certain to touch reality, and hence we must be skeptical about any skepticism with regard to this natural language and its essential concepts." But even the concepts of the most natural language are nevertheless constrained by the logic that rules any language. Eventually, we forget that language is not experience but is a selective description and a basically inaccurate, biased description, at that: ". . . we have to remember that what we observe is not natural itself but nature exposed to our method of questioning."

Another physicist, Bridgman, comments:

It has always been a major bewilderment to me to understand how anyone can experience such a common-place event as an automobile going up the street and seriously maintain that there is identity of structure of this continually flowing, dissolving and reforming thing, and the language that attempts to reproduce it with discrete units, tied together by remembered conventions.

An essential distinction between language and experience is that language separates out from the living matrix little bundles and freezes them; in doing this it produces something totally unlike experience, but nevertheless useful. That is, language as language is divorced from the *activity* which is the basal property of all our experience.

Thus, not only do we grant our symbols more reality than the experience that underlies them, but the abstract arrangements of those symbols and concepts create a picture of the world that is grossly in error. For example, we see boundaries where there are none. Your skin is in exchange with the blood and air. It excretes your wastes and absorbs the sun. You see it as a line—stable, fixed, a separation—only because the clock of your perception ticks at a particular rate and the microscope of your eyes is adjusted with a particular lens. Look more closely at the skin and the boundary line dissolves. Speed up the camera and the skin changes steadily like a sunset. Do you regard the sunset as an object? Only when it's frozen in a photo or a painting. Otherwise, when you stand beneath the late-afternoon sky and experience the vast incandescence of reddening light, you are aware of change and color sliding inexorably toward darkness.

How stable are the mountains! Yet set your movie camera to take one picture in a hundred years and the mountains will flow like ocean waves.

Where do you stand in the infinite scale of time and space? Look behind you, as time slows; the world congeals in static shapes. Look ahead in quickening time; forms dissolve in motion. Shrinking space discloses atomic speed; infinite distance shows a single point of light. In quickening time and microscopic space, the biological body loses all form: "As a result of its metabolism, which is characteristic of every living organism, its components are not the same from one moment to the next. Living forms are not in being, they are happening." Bones and muscles are not more fixed than blood: "What are called structures are slow processes of long duration; functions are quick processes of short duration. If we say that a function, such as the contraction of a muscle, is performed by a structure, it means that a quick and short process wave is superimposed on a long-lasting and slowly running wave." (Bertalanffy.) Shift our scale and the "inorganic" enters the stream of life. Our world is a world of gradients, not boundaries. Activity, change, and process are the "substance" of our world.

Scientists tell us now that their truth is relative, and, in important respects, their earlier "truth" has led us astray.

Consider Time:

> The time of the mathematician seems to have got itself ineradicably embedded in the thinking of modern civilization, for apparently we all nearly always think of time as a homogeneous and unlimited one-dimensional sequence, all past time on one side, all future time on the other, separated by the present which is in continuous motion from past to future. What could be more unlike the time of experience, apprehended with true freshness, which consists of a blurred sequence of memories, culminating in the budding and unfolding present?   [Bridgman.]

Consider Matter and the Particle that is supposed to compose it:

> According to modern mechanics [field theory], each individual particle of the system, in a certain sense, at any

one time, exists simultaneously in every part of the space occupied by the system. This simultaneous existence applies not merely to the field of force with which it is surrounded, but also its mass and charge.

Thus, we see that nothing less is at stake here than the concept of the particle—the most elementary concept of classical mechanics. We are compelled to give up the earlier essential meaning of this idea; only in a number of special border-line cases can we retain it.   [Planck.]

Before Clerk Maxwell, people conceived of physical reality—insofar as it is supposed to represent events in nature—as material points, whose changes consist exclusively of motions. . . . After Maxwell they conceived physical reality as represented by continuous fields, not mechanically explicable. . . . This change in the conception of reality is the most profound and fruitful one that has come to physics since Newton.   [Einstein.]

Consider Causality:

The objective world simply *is*, it does not *happen*. Only to the gaze of my consciousness, crawling along the life-line of my body, does a section of the world come to life as a fleeting image in space which continually changes in time.
                                            [Weyl.]

In man's brief tenancy on earth he egocentrically orders events in his mind according to his own feelings of past, present and future. But except on the reels of one's own consciousness, the universe, the objective world of reality, does not "happen"—it simply exists. It can be encompassed in its entire majesty only by a cosmic intellect. [Barnett.]

Concepts that we created to be our instruments in managing the world have become our masters: the tail wags the dog.

We are so under the sway of our cerebral Frankenstein that we usually do not perceive the difference between our phenomenal world—the world of being—and our meaning world. So as we live, we shroud the world in the gauze of our abstractions. This dome of abstractions, like an old-fashioned cake cover, encloses reality. It does so by altering our perception to fit our concepts, by selecting from the stimulus array that which our ideas expect, and by trapping much of our attention in the colorless monologue of our thoughts. As a result, we see only the world's shadowed outline. What is the world like when we lift that cover? Quite different, say the physicists, and the mystics, too. A contemporary sorcerer, Carlos Castaneda, has described "stopping the world," ceasing the activity whereby we create our conceptual gauze. When the conceptual activity stops, the phenomenal world breaks through, vivid and flowing:

> I turned around and examined an extraordinarily new world. The lines were visible and steady even if I looked away from the sun.
>
> I stayed on the hilltop in a state of ecstasy for what appeared to be an endless time, yet the whole event may have lasted only a few minutes, perhaps only as long as the sun shone before it reached the horizon, but to me it seemed an endless time. I felt something warm and soothing oozing out of the world and out of my own body. I knew I had discovered a secret. It was so simple. I experienced an unknown flood of feelings. Never in my life had I had such a divine euphoria, such peace, such an encompassing grasp, and yet I could not put the discovered

secret into words, or even into thoughts, but my body knew it.

Rebellion begins with the realization that you are in that conceptual and perceptual cage of your own making. The cage has covered you. Realizing that, you need not be gulled into buying shadows. Anxiety, loneliness, and death, the monster companions of man, are a product of your abstractions. Experience does not contain them. They are born in thought and memory, never in the Now. Bridgman writes: ". . . our insistent attempt to visualize death as some sort of experience is set against our intellectual realization that death is not experience. I suppose that our inability to think of death except in terms of experience has had more social consequences than any other vagary of the human mind." Without the concept of the object self, there is no loneliness. Without the phantoms of imagination, anxiety retreats and disappears. Time, Death, and Self have no power, except that which you confer upon them. Reclaim your power. They are servants, unworthy to command. It's been a swindle, all along.

"You've duped yourself. What made you give your power to The Boss?"

"Well, he's the boss! If I don't, he'll fire me."

"What then?"

"I'll die! I won't have any money and I'll starve, my family, too."

"You're smart enough to keep away from that. You'd find a way to get some food."

"There aren't any jobs."

"What do you want to do?"

"Man, I've got to eat."

"What else have you tried to do?"

"I haven't had the chance; these are hard times."

The conversation could go on a long time. Paralysis scents the air, plus helplessness and fear. The questions seem unfair at first, the answers obvious, and yet you sense a squirming and a sliding, a sideways glancing of the eyes, as you abandon one outpost after another, always in retreat, defending: "What can I do?"—the battle cry of dependency. Who is that person sneaking through the grass, scurrying through your mind, throwing back plaintive justifications to hamper pursuit? Haven't you noticed him before? You've paid him good wages to sit by your door making sure you're not disturbed by certain visitors. Now get him by the collar and hold him! Grab his chin and turn his head to face you (even then he looks away).

"Who's paying you off? What's his name?"

"Ah, give me a break, please—I'm afraid to be alone."

"Who said you'd be alone?"

"They all did. They said if I didn't join, they'd throw me out in no-man's-land and let me die."

"What no-man's-land?"

"There—outside the walls."

"What's it like?"

"How do I know? I haven't been there, but everybody knows it's hell."

And so you drop the wretch and turn away, struck by that

last phrase, "Everybody knows it's hell." Isn't it strange? No one in the city has passed those walls and yet they know it's hell. You were told that, too, remember? Your parents, warning you of destitution and abandonment: the old fears, back through the generations.

You learned from childhood, the terror of the nights so filled with your own frightened passions. And all those times your mother disappeared and you felt hunger and pain, without defense. And then, when she returned, it was so comforting being held while the soft voice murmured of the dangers outside parental arms. In elementary school, there was the punishment of isolation. Dunce! Sit in the corner! Later on, in high school, at the dance, you could stand by the wall and learn what it's like not to be chosen, not to be one of the crowd.

The needs of the child are preserved intact and used to establish laws for adult years, as if the needs were still the same. Societies, groups of every sort, conspire to a single overriding plan: preserve the group. "No member is allowed to leave; it weakens us!" So you are bribed (we'll comfort you), and threatened (leave and we'll kill you), and trained (serve your country, for in unity there is strength). All the institutions sing the same song: "You need us. Outside our sheltering walls is loneliness and death. Be one of us and we'll take care of you." From the United States of America to the latest yoga commune, no one gets to leave scot-free. "Insane," "bum," "commie," "freak," or "uptight," "fascist," "middle class": those are the clothes the Other wears. Take your pick; they smell the same and carry the same tag: Outsider. No hunting license required, no limit, take by any means: Thorazine, jail, contempt, and spit. Eat 'em up, lock 'em up. "Let 'em know that we won't stand their kind here!" "They put out bad vibes." "Serves them right!" "That'll teach 'em."

You've seen a lot of examples paraded down the main street of our town, or given the treatment in the ashram, in the newspapers and the neighborhood bar, and in the country club and the convention and Local Ordinance Number 666. Yes, indeed, they teach, "Outside the walls is hell!"

But what is it really like outside the walls? Suppose it isn't bad at all, suppose it is green grass and soft breezes, lots of sun and good things to eat? After all, some people have gone outside and said it's fine, even better than behind the wall. Of course, they're crazy—mystics, you know, foreign freaks mostly; what do they know without science training? Still, why not take a look? Rebel that far; consider that out there "alone" might be nicer than you have dreamed. What have you to lose? It's gotten awful stuffy in the town and there are rumors of a plague. Time to leave.

> Shibli was asked:
> "Who guided you in the Path?"
> He said: "A dog. One day I saw him, almost dead with thirst, standing by the water's edge.
> "Every time he looked at his reflection in the water he was frightened, and withdrew, because he thought it was another dog.
> "Finally, such was his necessity, he cast away fear and leapt into the water; at which the 'other dog' vanished.
> "The dog found that the obstacle, which was himself, the barrier between him and what he sought, melted away.

"In this same way my own obstacle vanished, when I knew it was what I took to be my own self. And my Way was first shown to me by the behavior of—a dog." [Shah.]

When fear departs, the encircling army melts away, but ignorance may still remain. There is much to learn. There is also much to do.

14.

Quitting

One time, not too long ago, I was discontented, agitated, and depressed. Something was wrong but I didn't know what it was, so I decided to go into the woods and think. I followed a trail along a stream bed that led through a spacious world of trees, with huge boulders and mossy banks, which created a succession of pictures, very composed and still. I walked, noticing the beauty, but my distress continued, as if hiking with me on a parallel trail. Finally, I stopped, sat upon the ground, and rested, gazing rather blankly before me. I was enclosed by trees that sheltered everything beneath them, creating a roof of green leaves and light in place of the sky.

A fantasy came to my mind. I saw myself as a troubled, intense, and angry young man who had gone to see a Teacher. I told him of my disgust with the world, how people hurt each other, did stupid things, and wouldn't listen when you offered help. No matter what I did, I told him, the same old thing happened, and even when things seemed to improve a little, sooner or later they went right back to where they were before.

Parents abused their children, creating more parents who would abuse their children and on . . . and on. People were obstinate and self-centered and kept ruining every chance they had. The misery of the world kept increasing, not decreasing, and Buddha and Christ have made no difference. Education hasn't made any difference, nothing makes any difference—it gets worse and worse, and more and more horrible.

The Teacher listened. Then he asked, "You hate the world?"

"Yes, I hate it, it's so mean and stupid, it destroys everything; and the more beautiful something is, the quicker it will destroy it. I'm fed up, I've had it. I don't know what to do now, there seems no point to anything, and I feel awful!"

The Teacher was silent for a while and then he said, "I have an idea of something that might help you, but I'm afraid it may prove too severe a task for you."

"No it won't, not after all the things I've done, how hard I've worked, how desperate I am. I care nothing about myself now. No matter how difficult or painful your task might be, I'd do it if I thought there was some hope."

"Very well," said the Teacher, "but I'm afraid it may be too difficult for you. It is this: Whatever you do you must enjoy, or you may not do it. No matter what it is, if you find that you are not enjoying it, you must stop right at that moment. It doesn't matter if you are driving your car, or eating, or doing your work, or doing anything else. If you are not enjoying it, you may not do it. It is up to you to find a way to enjoy anything that you do. Nothing is exempt: you may have to give up your work, you may have to stop in the middle of the street, you may look to others like an idiot, and you may sit on the floor and starve to death, but unless you enjoy whatever you're doing you may not do it. Do you understand?"

For a moment the young man's eyes were wide, incredulous, then they narrowed and his brow wrinkled in annoyance and disbelief. "That's impossible!" he exclaimed. "No one can enjoy everything and, besides, there are damn few things that are enjoyable. You're trying to trick me or having a joke!"

The Teacher smiled. "I was afraid it would be too difficult for you, and now you see what I mean. Nevertheless, I know of nothing else that would be of help to you. You must go away now. See if you can do it for a year and then come back."

A year later the young man returned. His face was open and glowing. "Good," said the teacher. "Now that you love the world, perhaps you can be of some use to it."

When I returned home from my day in the woods, I told my daughter the fantasy I had had. She said, "Do it! Do it for a year and then we'll celebrate." And so I did and I learned that I could enjoy anything. Then, after a while, I would forget. Sometimes, enjoying things no longer seemed so important. It had become my choice, a choice of how I wanted to be at any particular time, depending on my purpose. Often I forgot about enjoying things because I was just too busy.

How did I do it? I "stopped," "I quit." Each time I was unhappy I found that I was centered in my thoughts, my worries and concerns. For example, traveling to work, bored and restless in a long line of commuting cars speeding over the Golden Gate Bridge, I found that if I stopped and opened my eyes and ears and nose and touch (all the sensual channels), if I allowed that reality of smells and sounds and familiar color to fill the space of my attention, displacing thoughts as if my mind were hollow, then, with "me" gone, the sensate world entered suddenly, like an enormous guest who took up all the room but none of the space—and I enjoyed it. It wasn't "happiness"—happiness comes from me; enjoyment is in the being of the outside world, when it comes inside. Enjoyment comes with the flavor of the thing; it came with the car's qualities, its metal life, its special presence, noisy voice, strong being, hurtling character, the comfort of the seats, and the slanted shape of the glass. Its being spoke in sensual words and in something else more direct that senses. Around the car, the bridge unrolled, sending me an iron message, gray beneath the red and cold, yet soft and telling me its self. Nothing different than it is, nothing special. It's always there, waiting outside for me to open the door of my room and ask it in.

Do you know what I mean? Possibly not. You may be out of practice—so let me show you.

Consider: How long do you work? Eight hours? Not likely. Chances are you work every minute you're awake, and part-time while you're asleep. Consider all the orders you receive and all the ways you labor to meet the stream of commands. From your boss: "Finish today"; from yourself: "Make it neat"; from your leg: "I hurt—move!"; from the waiter: "Choose"; from a sign: "Buy me"; from a centerfold: "Screw me"; from the radio: "Remember this!"; from your spouse:

"Listen to me"; from your mind: "How?"; from your desires: "Fantasize"; from your fears: "Worry"; from your skin: "Scratch me"; from your car: 'Fix me"; from your room: "Clean me"; from your mind: "Talk with me"; from the golf club: "Swing me"; from a bottle: "Drink me"; from a problem: "Solve me"; and even from your vacation: "Enjoy me!"

Would you like to try quitting? You may never have done it before, never really *taken* time—any amount—just for you. You may never have said, "The next ten minutes are just for 'me,' " and stopped doing. Consider: ten full minutes in which to be aware, just for yourself, not doing anything, just being aware of your existence. Do you know what it is like to stop and give it all to yourself, to have the whole world just for you for as long as ten minutes? Find out. Try it now. Realize that no matter what problems are facing you and no matter what work you have to do or what people need you or what your body wants, for ten minutes there is nothing you *must* do. That's true. Realistically, no matter what your situation is right now, it can wait for ten minutes. The Bump may be coming, but the next ten minutes can be yours.

So set the alarm clock or ask someone else to let you know when the time is up so you don't even have to worry about that. Then quit. Sit comfortably. You needn't be solemn. You don't even have to close your eyes. Just quit. Feel how tired you are of saluting all those commands, or placating all those anxious messengers, so threatening, so seductive with their flattery and their bribes. Rebel. Does your foot hurt? Say to it, "To hell with you, I won't move!" Does your nose itch? "Sorry—go scratch yourself." In the middle of a thought you may suddenly realize that you've been thinking—well, just sag inside, let go of the thought and drop it to the floor. It's too much work to finish the thought, too much effort even to be annoyed, just too much. But don't go to sleep; that would be a swindle, that's what they're always doing. Every time you start to stop and see what it's like, they send you to sleep so you never get to know. This time quit *and* stay awake. Be curious: What is my experience when I stop doing? What is it like when I'm just being? Try it now. Just ten minutes. Stop reading. Stop. Quit now.

*

What was it like? You probably didn't stop just now, but kept on reading. You may have felt that you didn't have time, that you wanted to finish. That's the whole point: you are driven. So stop now and do it. Even if you have done "meditation" and think you know all about quitting, it is important that you stop—now—and do it, anyway. Don't go on reading. "Quit" now, for ten minutes, right where you are.

*

You may have found a world emerges that seems different. When the outward pressure of your mind relaxes, it leaves space that can be filled. Don't be afraid. Let the world move in and fill that space. See what it's like. Savor the color and the fragrance. Experience the rich, massive presence of the emerging world. Later, realize that Time was gone and so was your personality. Some part of self may have stayed to register anxiety or ask questions in your mind, but only from the back row. Satisfaction is the main event. How complete is the moment world! When you let it in, comparison collapses, for memory is gone, displaced by the fullness of the chair, the tree, the air, the sounds. You have been peering out the door at the world and now, in the twinkling of an eye, the world jumps into the room. Let it stay. Get acquainted with your guest. He won't stay too long; he's very sensitive to the host's concerns and will be gone before you voice the thought. Enjoy him. Be entertained. Even rest your head a while on his strong shoulder. Then you can come back to thinking, to doing.

That's how it seems to me, when I quit. You will have your own description. Back and forth you go, from being to doing, the two realms complementary, side by side—a biphasic world.

Want to try it again? Go ahead.

*

Once, in a Zen sesshin, after five days of focusing on my elusive, disappearing, watching self, I let go. Before that, during the first few days, the Zen master had said, "Show me yourself, find it, look for it, and bring it to me!" I tried. It can't be done. You may try, too. Twist and turn as fast as you can, you cannot see the eye of your awareness. As you struggle, as you watch the contents of your mind, every thought and every feeling, separation grows. You realize you are not them. You, the watcher, become more clear. And so you turn to find the watcher; and there is nothing here. Fear rushes to defend the empty citadel. Demons huff and puff in blustering dance. Just sit. Is it so bad, not being there? Touch a toe in the water; see, not so bad. A little longer, now. . . . Okay? Look around a little. You've been holding your breath—relax. Ready to jump in?

We chanted in the early morning. The words were printed black on large sheets of paper that we held before our eyes. Day by day, the words acquired life and vividness, until that morning of the fifth day they marched across the page not needing me at all. The world existed and I did not need to be. "Let go!" it whispered in my ear. "Disappear—the world will still be here, let it be without you, see what it's like when you aren't here; let go, let go, jump! Die."

Okay.

At the moment that I let go and vanished from the world, it changed. Abruptly, sharply, suddenly, at the moment of my "death," the world was something else—transfigured. All the students, robed in black, were Buddhas, perfect, radiating their perfection in awesome beauty. The bell sounded and the tone, like full silver, shone, pulsed, and vibrated from the heart of the bell, sounding its name. All was transfigured, godlike, fourth-dimensional.

I don't know how long it lasted. We rose and walked in line from the hall. Outside the birds spoke their note, their being-ness shimmered in the sound. As I walked, it all faded, and when I reached the cabins, it was gone.

I don't know what it really means, except the suddenness stays in my memory. Exactly when the self was gone, the radiant world appeared. They didn't overlap. The world emerged when I left. Well, who was there? Something remained to be the vantage point in space and time. Something experienced the room and moved outside. No one saw me disappear; my body stayed intact before the eyes of the man who was chanting behind me. What happened? I can't imagine. Psychologically, I "left" the world, relinquished my existence, and at that exact moment the world changed.

When you "quit," a short while back, did you feel the same—in a minor way? Were there moments when time had stopped, self-consciousness was gone, and everything was Now—as you realized only later when your thoughts and you and time and restlessness had returned? The hand is open or the hand is closed, you cannot "keep" the world of the open hand; the closing action of your mind's hand transforms you and the world. You cannot "know" it and have it at the same time, for the "knowing" needs a "you" to know. Now appears only when you leave. Perhaps that's why we seldom stay long—in the Now. We miss our object self.

The action mode and the receptive mode create two worlds. In one, the object self rules, served by linear time and thought, dedicated to control, but spawning anxiety. In the other, beyond self, perception replaces thought and Now replaces time. In that world, receiving is the goal, allowing the means; satisfaction results, and nourishment as well. We live in both worlds but possess only one, for it is the self that possesses. And so we easily forget that the other world's there; we fill in the gaps between the world of self with memory and finally believe that the object world is continuous, unbroken, supreme. Yet, if we quit, if we stop, Past, Now, and the Future can sound in harmony. That complete music restores the soul, for what was held apart is brought together, allowing selfless action and purposeful existence.

Have you ever been a "channel," performing action with such effectiveness and grace, with such a matching of need and answer that "It wasn't me that did it!" arises in your mind? "Allah did it!" exclaimed the runner, fresh after twenty-six miles, doing push-ups in exuberance, the gold Olympic medal his, but not his, he said. Or "the perfect hour" of the therapist, when the action is a dance between two minds in tune. "Like a spider upon the water, his mind moves upon silence," said Yeats of Michelangelo. "Allah did it!" because we think we are the object self that consciously controls. When the worlds unite in harmony, the flow of power that results feels different from the self that only knows the strain of willing. When you let go the object self, when the "ego" is not you, perhaps you'll know that power to be your own, for you'll feel no boundaries to restrict you from your rightful home.

15.

Realistic Action

"Be realistic!" Who hasn't received that reprimand? Usually it is an exhortation to be more cynical or more suspicious, to pay more attention to the money or the impossibility of an ideal. Sometimes the rebuke is needed, for our wishes may intoxicate us and clouds of fantasy can surround our heads, obscuring the ground. But "Be realistic" often means, "Don't let your guard down, get what you can; ideals are for suckers and the world is full of wolves. Be practical!"

The successful man of business is the model we are given for being "practical." Politicians come close behind; both scorn "romantic dreamers." The military, the bankers, the public officials, the corporate executives—the men of power— they are The Realists. Although there has been evidence enough that something is missing, that such "realism" produces wars, economic depressions, and a large number of Miniver Cheevys who blow their brains out in one way or another, the man of power has retained his authority as the voice of realism. On the other hand, the ethics and points of view expressed in religious and mystical traditions are regarded as practical only on Sundays, and not really practical, even then: "All that's okay theoretically, but the world is different and you've got to hustle to survive!" These words may be a caricature, but this view has penetrated us so deeply that most people carry around their own interior voice that pounces on deviant thoughts, labeling them "romantic," "impractical," "mystical," "magical," "crazy." The voice of "realism" comes down like a whip, keeping us in line.

We listen to that voice not only because we have been trained to it, but because there is much in our thinking that is magical indeed. The wishes, fears, and passions of our childhood persist and live again in our behavior. And the laws of object logic are needed to survive. No matter how free your spirit, you cannot fly from the tenth floor of a building; you will fall and die. Respond to every outstretched hand and soon your own will be outstretched.

Nevertheless, something is clearly wrong with the old way. The action mode of thought, perception, and activity is no longer realistic by itself; conquering the object world, we stand in the shadow of species death. It is men of business, politics, and war who have led the long march and are now openly confused, uncertain, and frightened; the line of their march is straight for the cliff.

Most scientists have erred, as well. Too arrogant in intellect, they discarded what they could not think, labeling it "unreal." But they have begun to see that error and they speak now in other terms.

The conclusions of a multidisciplinary research group:

Numerous problems today have no technical solution. Examples are the nuclear arms race, racial tensions, and unemployment. Even if society's technological progress fulfills all expectations, it may very well be a problem with no technical solution, or the interaction of several such problems, that finally brings a disastrous end to population and capital growth.

A professor of electrical engineering, Willis Harman:

. . . hardly a task can be imagined for which a technology cannot be developed if resources are devoted to it and sufficient time is allowed. Hardly a task, that is, except solution of the huge societal problems that now confront us, and which seem in considerable measure to be a product of our technological prowess. Perhaps a third frontier is the inward one—the frontier of the vast inner space of consciousness. And perhaps it is here that we must turn to find the eventual resolution of these problems that so perplex us.

No technical solutions! The Western genie hangs his head, his powers of possession, of conquest and control, of building and destruction now useless, worse than useless.

What is needed?

The research group proposes:

. . . trading certain human freedoms, such as producing unlimited numbers of children or consuming uncontrolled amounts of resources, for other freedoms, such as relief from pollution and crowding and the threat of collapse of the world's system. It is possible that new freedoms might also arise—universal and unlimited education, leisure for creativity and inventiveness, and, most important of all, the freedom from hunger and poverty enjoyed by such a small fraction of the world's people today.

Hell or paradise would appear to lie within the realm of our choice. Our choice, however, depends on our values, and our values depend upon our outlook, our concepts, on the way we view ourselves and others; it is not a technical problem.

A former physicist, now futurist, J. R. Platt, makes a similar point:

> We may be facing a decade or more of disasters, as our older institutions and nation-state structures are forced to deal with the new global crises. Our ability to handle these crises depends upon leadership and commitment and organizational structure and our ability to make necessary changes fast enough. But it probably also depends in a crucial way on how rapidly we all begin to accept and practice certain concepts about our relation to each other and to the world, concepts that are essential for global cooperation and survival. . . .

What concepts?

A naturalist, Aldo Leopold, speaking almost thirty years ago:

> We abuse land because we regard it as a commodity belonging to us. When we see land as a community to which we belong, we may begin to use it with love and respect. There is no other way for land to survive the impact of mechanized man, nor for us to reap from it the esthetic harvest it is capable of. . . .
>
> That land is a community is a basic concept of ecology, but that land is to be loved and respected is an extension

of ethics. That land yields a cultural harvest is a fact long known, but latterly often forgotten.

The concepts are those of community and oneness, based on the perception of oneself in kinship with the earth, rather than as its conquerer; of feeling connected to a thousand generations of human, animal, vegetable, and even mineral forms, stretching far behind us in evolutionary time and with a destiny that stretches far beyond us into the future. In the usual random, mechanistic, aggressive world view, the long-term goal of the evolution of our species hardly seems practical when compared to the need to invest in a retirement plan, or to build a house; anxiety tips the scales forever in the direction of short-term profit. "If I don't do it, the next guy will"; there is truth in that prediction. Yet such "practical" advice is leading us and our children to utter desolation.

J. R. Platt, again:

> We are passing through a philosophical and religious transformation in this generation, a transformation consistent with our new scientific knowledge as well as with our new awareness of inner human meaning and outer global responsibility. It is a transformation that is even more remarkable and more necessary than the astonishing technological transformation and social transformations of our time. It is only on some new philosophical and religious foundation of this kind that any viable society of our children and grandchildren can be built.

A change in our customary world view is now a practical necessity, and that change would seem to require a different experience of one's personal self, of time, of the living world. It is not a matter of technologies, of finding new ways to manipulate the environment, but of a change in perception, leading to a change in values. The values needed are congruent with the assertions of mystics, "romantic dreamers," people ordinarily regarded as completely impractical.

Mystical perceptions always undergo translation, and translation leads to error, but a consistent message does emerge from many different texts: 1. the value of surrender to the natural flow of the world; 2. the futility of pursuing material satisfactions; 3. the possibility of attaining a mode of existence superior to the one in which we usually live; and 4. the unknowable presence or force that is no-thing, defined by negatives, since it is not part of the object world and yet is perceptible. That "God," that "Love," is immanent in every man and in every thing. We are waves, mystics say, and like waves not different from the ocean. Yet who *knows* that this is true? Who knows what these words, derived from objects, mean when applied beyond the object world? It is difficult for us to grasp, centered as we are in the action mode. Thus, "surrender" is distasteful and "no-thing" appears to be a joke.

The course of our learning from womb to adulthood has been a path of adaptation to objects. We learned to use the object world by becoming objects ourselves. Having created an object self, we have defended that same self, and now "surrender" or "selflessness" feels like a loss. To surrender to something other than yourself, as mystics advise, suggests passivity and the threat of slavery.

A thousand tyrants have invited surrender, and history is

witness to the perils of relinquishing one's will. China is powerfully self-sufficient, but the Western observer is often chilled, uneasy by what the Chinese, with admirable selflessness, have surrendered. The most precious jewel of modern civilization is the possibility of freedom, the freedom to be what we really are, in its unique form, and to be that with full strength and with our full heritage. Uniqueness and autonomy should not be surrendered.

Our fear of "surrender" arises from a confusion of modes, a judging of one realm by the concepts of another. Our education in the action mode has pre-empted our minds, narrowing our lives; meanwhile, the experience of beyond self is minimal and overbalanced by the action mode. Although that mode has made possible freedom from material needs and from disease, it has also brought us to the edge of disaster. That is understandable: we have lost our organismic balance. The receptive mode, the intuitive mode, the allowing mode, is needed now for our survival. It has always been there, perhaps provided for a time of need—which is now—but we have not used it. We have tolerated living in an odd, abstract world, constructed and maintained by all those forces of indoctrination to which we subscribe, knowingly or not: schools, family training, college, newspapers, job requirements—all flying the flag of self, of acquisition, of socially approved conquest and control. That system is no longer enough; we need a different kind of action, a new realism.

The world ship is sinking. There is no time to free ourselves unless freeing ourselves helps the world at the same time. Can we do that? How?

THE THREE PRISONERS

After the death of Rabbi Uri of Strelisk, who was called
the Seraph, one of his hasidim came to Rabbi Bunam and
wanted to become his disciple. Rabbi Bunam asked: "What
was your teacher's way of instructing you to serve?"

"His way," said the hasid, "was to plant humility in
our hearts. That was why everyone who came to him,
whether he was a nobleman or a scholar, had first to fill
two large buckets at the well in the market place, or to do
some other hard and menial labor in the street."

Rabbi Bunam said: "I shall tell you a story. Three men,
two of them wise and one foolish, were once put in a
dungeon black as night, and every day food and eating
utensils were lowered down to them. The darkness and the
misery of imprisonment had deprived the fool of his last
bit of sense, so that he no longer knew how to use the
utensils he could not see. One of his companions showed
him, but the next day he had forgotten again, and so his
wise companion had to teach him continually.

"But the third prisoner sat in silence and did not bother
about the fool. Once the second prisoner asked him why
he never offered his help.

" 'Look!' said the other. 'You take infinite trouble and
yet you never reach the goal, because every day destroys
your work. But I sit here and try to think out how I can
manage to bore a hole in the wall so that the light and
sun can enter, and all three of us can see everything.' "

[Buber.]

He sits and thinks in isolation: it is not enough. The other
teaches the fool: it is not enough; the fool does not learn.
None of the three works toward escape and freedom. None
of the three knows how.

But if they worked together, couldn't they escape? Couldn't the fool provide shoulders on which one wise man could stand, whose own shoulders might be the base from which the third could reach the opening above? Or perhaps they'd share utensils and, together, dig through the wall to freedom. The strength and skill of each need to be combined in the service of the larger goal.

We are blind and crazy most of the time, living in dungeons—although we do not know it. Our abstractions swirl through our heads, creating phantom worlds of their own in which we stumble around enchanted, seeking to escape by constructing more rooms within more mental rooms. The rooms are our theories, theories of all kinds: what is good, what is man, time, death, and god. Most theories were learned so long ago we've forgotten they are theories; we think they're real. Yet every thought we have is unreal, a selection, an abstraction. Inside the abstract rooms we cannot see the world. It is a perceptual problem; the answer is not more thought but more perception.

Watching is the key. Watch what draws you back into the prison rooms. What holds you there, like a spider's thread? "Attachment to objects makes men blind and deaf," said Mohammed. Notice the attachments, see where the strands are stuck to objects (money, youth, approval, pleasure), trace them back inside. There is a place where the web collects. When I look inside and see its shape, I realize that it's the personal self, the phantom built of my desires: my memories, emotions, virtues, skills, the color of my hair—everything I've won and built and call myself, the object I was taught was me. The bonds of attachment, the spider's silk, fan out from "me" to the things of the world.

We have used the action mode to spin the web, and we are caught. Yet action is not bad. The action mode preserves our biological self; with it we preserve others. We need the action mode to play our role in man's journey, but it must give way to action of a different kind. So the Vedas declare: "It is not action that brings suffering but the greediness of the mind for the result, that strengthens our bondage in the world."

Desire sustains the object self and feeds it; desire is the wish to have. To have we must be objects. After all, there must be something that can *have* what is desired; that object is the personal self. There we stand, object to object; and then the trouble starts. Whatever we desire, we must get and keep; there is disappointment from expectations and there is fear of loss, "me" and "my" object must be preserved. And objects become hated from fear as they are loved from desire. So we suffer from desire; we are objectified.

"I want and so I act. What else can there be?"

Something else. First stop having. Step away from it, as if you were walking through a store, enjoying the sight of all the merchandise, but declining to be encumbered. There is the salesman; he holds out the thing you want. See it glitter! Beautiful! But it is heavy to carry; it becomes a strain. Decline. Let the interior muscles ease, your hands fall to your sides, resting there. Look, admire, and walk away.

"What happens then?"

When you give up having, your problems disappear. Is that

a strange idea, impossible, absurd? Try it; you can do it. Step aside. Give it up. Let it go.

"But what is left? What remains?"

Experiencing. Acting. And something more.

"Why would I want to act at all?"

You will act. The present moment calls us, what is needed can guide our way. The flow of things provides direction if we're aligned. Relinquishing having, we are free to feel the current and, like swimmers, be carried and act at the same time.

The old traditions speak of service: performing of an action without thought of gain. Not because it's Good, but because the thought of gain spins another strand of silk, anchoring you to your object self. You are freed when you serve a task, doing what is needed, what the moment calls for. Working "selflessly," you walk away from the spider's web.

MUDDY ROAD

Tansan and Ekido were once traveling together down a muddy road. A heavy rain was still falling.

Coming around a bend, they met a lovely girl in a silk kimono and sash, unable to cross the intersection.

"Come on, girl," said Tanzan at once. Lifting her in his arms, he carried her over the mud.

Ekido did not speak again until that night when they reached a lodging temple. Then he no longer could restrain himself. "We monks don't go near females," he told Tanzan, "especially not young and lovely ones. It is dangerous. Why did you do that?"

"I left the girl there," said Tanzan. "Are you still carrying her?" [Reps.]

Desires, fears, and hatred: with these the object self fastens us to other objects. The strands are invisible. To find them we must feel them. How can we feel them and trace them to their binding post, to cast them off, attaining freedom? Everyday life is our means, for our attachments happen every day. In all the little actions of our life, the self arises and binds us. Everyday life is the path. Our difficulties, our discomforts, our despair are signals that our object self has driven us to clutch a puff of smoke. Such suffering is not our essence, not our "tragic destiny"; it is the wasteful, grotesque product of an abstract world, our unseen insanity. Our everyday pain is a chance to see, and through seeing to become free.

Intuition tells us there is hell, purgatory, and heaven:

Hell is suffering without hope. Ignorant of the cause, we go around and around in a circle of cause and effect of our own making.

Purgatory is suffering through which we become free of suffering. In purgatory we use suffering as an occasion to learn. Understanding the cause of our suffering, we break the circle.

Heaven is freedom, harmony, love. Suffering is a function of self-concern. Having freed ourselves of self-concern, Heaven arises as our new being.

All three realms are present in our everyday life.

Everyday life is the path for us. Everyday life is the path for alleviating the misery of the world. Contemplation on a mountain top won't do. Squatting in one's corner of the dungeon won't do. The world needs you to work in it; you need the world to learn. Sacrifice? No. Somber toil? No. The joy of action; the high pleasure of selfless power; the exquisite, sensual delight of sanity? Yes! So, what do you say?

"What should I do?"

No! Don't say that. It kills it. It kills you. Asking that creates a state of consciousness from which nothing can be done. Experiment and see. Pretend to be asking someone, "What should I do?" Close your eyes and feel what asking that question does to you. Do it now. Stop reading, close your eyes, and ask, "What should I do?" (Try it now.)

*

What was it like? Did you feel uncertain, a little bewildered, forehead wrinkled slightly, eyes a little pinched, looking upward, plaintively, to someone else—waiting to be told? It's the old dependency poison seeping into every cell, deadening the energy of change.

"What should I do?"

You can always find someone who will reply:

"Join Zero Population Growth."

"Be more honest."

"There's nothing you can do; it's out of your hands!"

"Contribute."

"Boycott!"

"Stock up on food!"

"Buy a farm (don't forget the guns)."

"Move to New Zealand!"

Does that help? Imagine millions of people following those directions, scurrying like ants, swarming back and forth from New Zealand to the grocery store to a rally to a stiff drink to bed. No, it doesn't help.

"So what should I do?" The eyes roll up to heaven, the shoulders shrug, and helplessness, like a warm, soft shawl, wraps itself around the already snoring citizen.

It's a functional matter. "What should I do?" asks for help, and asking for help throws a switch on the organismic engine, readying it for that purpose. Helplessness has a function, and body and mind cooperate in the task of being cared for, of being helped. Being cared for is not bad; it is an activity, like any other. But "What should I do?" cannot lead you to realistic action in the world.

So ask a different question: "Where does my energy want to go?"

For that you turn inside, to yourself. You listen and feel . . . "Where does my energy want to go?" Unaccustomed to asking, you may not hear an answer. So try a fantasy: Imagine you are free and unafraid, completely unafraid—what would you want to do? Go ahead, close your eyes, imagine that your fear is gone and you are strong—what would you want to do? (Try the fantasy now.)

*

What came to mind? What did your energy show you? Was it something unreal? If it showed you pleasure, that's not bad. Pleasing yourself may be the first step, a test to know that you are free. If so, imagine next that you have had the pleasure and can have more, but what else would you want to do? What service is yours? What would be fun to try? What venture would call forth your strength in a joyful pouring out of all you have, the thing you'd want to try to do, if you were free, if you were unafraid? What action is yours?

So ask that question again: "Where does my energy want to go?" Close your eyes. Listen. Feel. Watch what you are shown.

Before his death, Rabbi Zusya said, "In the coming world, they will not ask me: 'Why were you not Moses?' They will ask me: 'Why were you not Zusya?' " [Buber.]

Conclusion

All these things have been true for me, have helped me stay afloat on the wild ocean of my life. They are truths about the human world. Yet they are perishable answers: they help only for a while and they carry me just so far. True as they may be, they have not been enough. For a long time, I continued seeking an end to my restlessness; my dissatisfaction could be lulled for a while but would return saying, "Something is still wrong." I needed solid ground under my feet, not emotions or "experiences" or more abstractions. These past few years my seeking has subsided, for I'm learning what it is I have to do, and as I do it the confusion of this world begins to clear. Let me tell you how this has happened. Realistically, you ought to know so you won't be misled. And it might apply to you.

I've been learning by reading teaching stories, like the ones I've shown you here. They've been prepared by a modern Sufi named Idries Shah. They're not secret; you can buy the books in many stores. The stories themselves are strange. Some are simple, some fantasy; some are rich, some are sparse. All are strangely powerful. They infiltrate invisibly, disappearing from my mind. Then a moment comes when they reappear, spring to sight, and show the motive of my thought and action in the everyday. They show me myself.

The stories are changing my life, my world. They seem to be templates, patterns that mirror patterns of deceit, subtle self-deceit that has clogged my vision so I cannot see. Bit by bit, vision improves and my life is clarified, like a foggy day clearing in patches, revealing glimpses of the sky.

There is a Teaching, the stories say, a science for knowing what we are and what we're for. It has worn a thousand costumes, to fit cultures of the past. The Teaching moves on, but its costumes remain behind, colorful shells, the life force gone. At present, old and interesting costumes abound, good for playing games, creating confusion. But the Teaching is still alive and here today, the stories say, invisible in contemporary clothes, specific for the time, the place, and the right people.

The stories work. I've been reading them three years, and I haven't met Idries Shah. It doesn't seem to matter. He's written his books for the Western mind that's bred to literature and intellect; he says our minds need preparation and the mode of teaching must be different from the mode that suited a peasant in Japan, an Arab in the Middle Ages, or a Jew in ancient Rome.

My life has been changing. Something is happening that is different from what went before, more direct, more powerful, freeing me in ways I do not notice at the time. Not "spiritual" in any sense I thought I knew that word. Yet it

150

feels like land after a shipwreck. Hard work—more hard than what has gone before. The effort my own; the subject my behavior and my thought: independence of a different kind. Hard work. The only kind that seems to meet the need for waking from our strange world dream.

THE MAGIC MONASTERY

A certain quiet dervish used often to attend the weekly meals given by a cultivated and generous man. This circle was known as "The Assembly of the Cultured."

The dervish never took part in the conversation, but simply arrived, simply shook hands with all present, seated himself in a corner, and ate the food provided.

When the meeting was over, he would stand up, say a word of farewell and thanks, and go his way. Nobody knew anything about him, though when he first appeared there were rumours that he was a saint.

For a long time the other guests thought that he must indeed be a man of sanctity and knowledge, and they looked forward to the time when he might impart some of his wisdom to them. Some of them even boasted of his attendance at their meetings to their friends, hinting at the special distinction which they felt in his presence.

Gradually, however, because they could feel no relationship with this man developing, the guests began to suspect that he was an imitator, perhaps a fraud. Several of them felt uncomfortable in his presence. He seemed to do nothing to harmonize himself with the atmosphere, and did not even contribute a proverb to the enlightened conversation which they had come to prize as a necessary part of their very lives. A few, on the other hand, became unaware that he was there at all, since he drew no attention to himself.

One day the dervish spoke. He said:

"I invite all of you to visit my monastery, tomorrow night. You shall eat with me."

This unexpected invitation caused a change in the opinions of the whole assembly. Some thought that the dervish, who was very poorly dressed, must be mad, and surely could provide them with nothing. Others considered his past behavior to have been a test. At last, they said to themselves, he would reward them for their patience in bearing with such dreary company. Still others said to one another:

"Beware, for he may well be trying to lure us into his power."

Curiosity led them all, including their host, to accept the hospitality.

The following evening the dervish led them from the house to a hidden monastery of such size and magnificence that they were dazed.

The building was full of disciples carrying out every kind of exercise and task. The guests passed through contemplation-halls filled with distinguished-looking sages who rose in respect and bowed at the dervish's approach.

The feast which they were given surpassed all powers of description.

The visitors were overwhelmed. All begged him to enroll them as disciples forthwith.

But the dervish would only say, to all their entreaties: "Wait until the morning."

Morning came and the guests, instead of waking in the luxurious silken beds to which they had been conducted the night before, clad in gorgeous robes, found themselves lying stiff and stark, dispersed on the ground within the stony confines of a huge and ugly ruin, on a barren mountainside. There was no sign of the dervish, of the beautiful arabesques, the libraries, the fountains, the carpets.

"The infamous wretch has tricked us with the deceits of sorcery!" shouted the guests. They alternately condoled with and congratulated one another for their sufferings and for having at last seen through the villain, whose enchantments obviously wore off before he could achieve his evil purpose, whatever that might be. Many of them attributed their escape to their own purity of mind.

But what they did not know was that, by the same means which he had used to conjure up the experience of the monastery, the dervish had made them believe that they were abandoned in a ruin. They were, in fact, in neither place.

He now approached the company, as if from nowhere, and said:

"We shall return to the monastery."

He waved his hands, and all found themselves back in the palatial halls.

Now they repented, for they immediately convinced themselves that the ruins had been the test, and that this monastery was the true reality. Some muttered:

"It is as well that he did not hear our criticisms. Even if he only teaches us this strange art, it will have been worth while."

But the dervish waved his hands again, and they found themselves at the table of the communal meal: which they had, in fact, never left.

The dervish was sitting in his customary corner, eating his spiced rice as usual, saying nothing at all.

And then, watching him uneasily, all heard his voice speak as if within their own breasts, though his lips did not move. He said:

"While your greed makes it impossible for you to tell self-deceit from reality, there is nothing real which a dervish can show you—only deceit. Those whose food is self-defeat and imagination can be fed only with deception and imagination."

Everyone present on that occasion continued to frequent the table of the generous man. But the dervish never spoke to them again.

After some time the members of the Assembly of the Cultured realized that his corner was now always empty.

[Shah.]

My intellect has helped to show me the bars of my cage of dreams, which it has helped create. It has not shown me the key in my hand with which I lock myself in, which I need to cease turning. The stories show me that. What may come next I do not know. I feel more sane and would not go back for any amount of "bliss" that I had felt before. Sanity is the finest pleasure I have known. So I work on myself, to reduce greed, vanity, and fear.

EXCLUSION

Rais El-Aflak, "The Lord of the Skies," who suddenly appeared in Afghanistan and then disappeared after giving a number of cryptic lectures, said:

"Almost all of the men who come to see me have strange imaginings about man. The strangest of these is the belief that they can progress only by improvement. Those who will understand me are those who realize that man is just as much in need of stripping off rigid accretions to reveal the knowing essence, as he is of adding anything.

"Man thinks always in terms of inclusion into a plan of people, teachings and ideas. Those who are really the Wise know that the Teaching may be carried out also by exclusion of those things which make man blind and deaf."

[Shah.]

No need to "improve" yourself, no need to accept stoically your "existential despair." No need to drink the poison of "Each person is alone." No need to swear allegiance to the strange world that you've been taught and learned: the road of time, isolation, meaninglessness, and the confinement of your consciousness to the little box, labeled with your name, out of which you peer. No need to push aside your inner sense that says, "Something is wrong."

The truth is very hopeful. Very strong. Very real.

"There is no cause for fear. It is imagination, blocking you as a wooden bolt holds the door. Burn that bar. . . ."

Reference Notes

Chapter 2: *LEARNING ABOUT REALITY*

Page:
7. *Slowly, we grow*: D. Hooker, cited in P. Greenacre, "The Biological Economy of Birth," *Psychoanalytic Study of the Child* 1 (1945): 36.
8. *If you tap*: D. Spelt, "The Conditioning of the Human Fetus in Utero," *Journal of Experimental Psychology* 38 (1948): 338–46.
8. *Microscopic studies show*: L. B. Arey, cited in Greenacre, op. cit., p. 37.
9. *The different subjects*: M. Clymes, cited in "The Mathematics of Emotions," *The New Scientist*, December 31, 1970, p. 580.
10. *Salamanders grow back*: Robert Becker, Carol Bachman, and Hugh Friedman, "The Direct Current Control System," *New York State Journal of Medicine* 62, no. 8 (April 1962): 1169–76.
10. *The serenity, agitation*: N. W. Sontag, "Differences in Modifiability of Fetal Behavior and Physiology," *Psychosomatic Medicine* 6 (1944): 151–54.
12. *They may be memories*: M. Straker, "Comparative Studies of the Effects of Normal and Caesarian Delivery upon Later Manifestations of Anxiety," *Comprehensive Psychiatry* 3, no. 2 (1962): 113–24.
12. *These "memories" were*: Stanislav Grof, *Realms of the Human Unconscious* (New York: The Viking Press, 1975).

Chapter 3: *LESSONS OUTSIDE THE WOMB*

Page:

16. *When adults, blind*: Marius Von Senden, *Space and Sight* (Glencoe, Illinois: Free Press, 1960).

16. *Finally, he opens*: Jean Piaget, *The Origins of Intelligence in Children*, 2d ed. (New York: International Universities Press, 1952), pp. 337–38.

16. *Those pattern modes*: Erik H. Erikson, *Childhood and Society* (New York: W. W. Norton, 1950).

17. *We pay a price*: Sunryu Suzuki, *Zen Mind, Beginner's Mind* (New York: Walker/Weatherhill, 1970), pp. 17–18.

17. *Color and texture*: David Shapiro, "A Perceptual Understanding of Color Response," in M. Rickers-Ovsiankina *Rorschach Psychology* (New York: John Wiley & Sons, 1960), pp. 154–201.

18. *Mother leaves, but*: Sigmund Freud, "A Metapsychological Supplement to the Theory of Dreams," *The Standard Edition of the Complete Psychological Works of Sigmund Freud*, vol. 14 (London: The Hogarth Press, 1957), p. 232.

18. *For the moment*: Dorothy Lee, "Codifications of Reality: Lineal and Non-Lineal," *Psychosomatic Medicine* 12, no. 2 (1950): 89–97.

18. "[Eighteen-month-old children]": Louise B. Ames, "The Sense of Self of Nursery School Children as Manifested by Their Verbal Behavior," *The Journal of Genetic Psychology* 81 (1952): 193–232.

19. ". . . even the sense": Arnold Gesell et al., *The First Five Years of Life: A Guide to the Study of the Pre-School Child* (New York: Harper & Row, 1940), p. 32.

19. "Child grabbed from": Ames, op. cit., p. 199.

19. "Pronouns, *mine, me, you*: Gesell, op. cit., p. 37.

Chapter 4: *THE ACTION MODE*

Page:

21. *Briefly, however, between*: Peter Wolff, "The Causes, Controls, and Organization of Behavior in the Neonate," *Psychological Issues* 5, no. 1 (17): 41–43.

21. *A mode of living*: Arthur Deikman, "Bimodal Consciousness," *Archives of General Psychiatry* 25 (December 1971): 481–89. Also in Robert E. Ornstein, ed., *The Nature of Human Consciousness* (San Francisco: W. H. Freeman and Company, 1973), pp. 67–86.

24. *Vision softens*: Arthur Deikman, "The Relationship Between EEG, EMG and Meditation," paper read at the Conference on Altered States of Consciousness and Suggestology, Pepperdine University, Los Angeles, May 2–4, 1975.

24. *I-Thou*: Martin Buber, *I and Thou* (New York: Charles Scribner's Sons, 1958).

25. "There was a time": William Wordsworth, "Intimations of Immortality from Recollections of Early Childhood," in *Complete Poetical Works of William Wordsworth* (New York: Houghton Mifflin, Riverside Press, Cambridge Edition, 1904), p. 353.

Chapter 5: CONSEQUENCES

Page:
28. *Others see your*: George Mead, *Mind, Self and Society* (Chicago: The University of Chicago Press, 1934).

33. *For some*: Leslie H. Faber, "Ours Is an Addicted Society," *New York Times Magazine*, 1966.

Chapter 6: SPIRITUAL DOORS

Page:
37. *Western scientists have*: R. Wallace, H. Benson, and A. Wilson, "A Wakeful Hypometabolic Physiologic State," *American Journal of Physiology* 221, no. 3 (1971): 795–99.

39. "If we keep": J. Clark and J. Skinner, eds., *Treatises and Sermons of Meister Eckhart* (New York: Harper & Row, 1958), p. 104.

39. "Binding the mind": James Woods, *The Yoga-System of Patanjali* (Cambridge, Mass.: The Harvard University Press, Harvard Oriental Series, 1914), p. 42.

39. "When this active effort": Dwight Goddard, *A Buddhist Bible*, 2d ed. (Thetford, Vt.: Dwight Goddard, 1938), p. 323.

39. "For if such": Walter Hilton, *The Scale of Perfection* (London: Burns and Coates, 1953), p. 380.
40. "Renunciation . . .": Sunryu Suzuki, lecture given at Zen Mountain Center, July 1968, *Wind Bell* 7, no. 28 (1968).
40. "He said that": Walpola Rahula, *What the Buddha Taught* (New York: Grove Press, 1962), pp. 1–2.
42. "There are perhaps": Sunryu Suzuki, *Zen Mind, Beginner's Mind* (New York: Walker/Weatherhill, 1970), p. 63.

Chapter 7: OTHER DOORS

Page:
47. "The Truth of Atman": Swami Nikhilananda, *The Upanishads*, vol. 1 (New York: Harper & Row, 1949), p. 112.
47. "Worship the guru": Swami Muktananda, *Guru* (New York: Harper & Row, 1971).
48. *The gaze will*: J. Allison, "Cognitive Structure and Receptivity to Low Intensity Stimulation," *Journal of Abnormal and Social Psychology* 67, no. 2 (1963) : 132–38.
49. *There are books*: Michael Murphy, *Golf in the Kingdom* (New York: The Viking Press, 1972) ; W. Timothy Gallwey, *The Inner Game of Tennis* (New York: Random House, 1974) ; George Leonard, *The Ultimate Athlete* (New York: The Viking Press, 1975).
50. *"Spiritual materialism"*: Chogyam Trungpa, *Cutting Through Spiritual Materialism* (Berkeley: Shambala, 1973), pp. 13–23.

Chapter 8: DEPENDENCY

Page:
54. "To study Buddhism": Dogen Zenji, "Shobogenzo: Genjo Koan" (T. Maezumi, trans.), *ZCLA Journal* 2, no. 4 (Fall 1972) : 3.
60. THE STORY OF THE CAPE: Martin Buber, *Tales of the Hasidim: Early Masters* (New York: Schocken Books, 1947), p. 286.
62. *So the badness*: W. R. D. Fairbain, cited in H. Guntrip, "The Therapeutic Factor in Psychotherapy," *British Journal of Medical Psychology* 26 (1953) : 128.

Chapter 9: *PSYCHOTHERAPY*

Page:
69. ALL YOU NEED: Idries Shah, *The Exploits of Mulla Nasrudin* (London: Jonathan Cape, 1966), p. 138.
70. "Someone said": Idries Shah, *Thinkers of the East* (London: Jonathan Cape, 1971), p. 137.
71. "When you feel": Ibid., p. 189.
76. THE FIFTIETH GATE: Buber, op. cit., p. 92.

Chapter 10: *THIRD-LEVEL SCHOOL*

Page:
82. *Depression Serves:* G. Engle and A. Schmale, "Conservation-Withdrawal: A Primary Regulatory Process for Organismic Homeostasis," in *Physiology, Emotion and Psychosomatic Illness,* London, CIBA Foundation Symposium, 1972, pp. 58–85.
82. *This theory is:* M. Reite et al., "Depression in Infant Monkeys: Physiologic Correlates," *Psychosomatic Medicine* 36, no. 4 (July-August 1974) : 363–67.
84. "Then the next stage": Chogyam Trungpa, *Cutting Through Spiritual Materialism* (Berkeley: Shambala, 1973), p. 144.
85. *We need that reassurance:* Douglas E. Harding, *On Having No Head* (New York: Harper & Row, Perennial Library, 1972).

Chapter 11: *THE PATH AS A MULTISTAGE ROCKET: A SPECULATION*

Page:
98. *You've heard the classic puzzles:* Paul Reps, ed., *Zen Flesh, Zen Bones* (Garden City: Anchor Books/Doubleday), pp. 119–20.

Chapter 12: *WATCHING*

Page:
101. "There is no cause": Idries Shah, *Caravan of Dreams* (London: The Octagon Press, 1968), p. 79.

Chapter 13: REBELLING

Page:

110. "The white matter": Liberato J. Didio, *Synopsis of Anatomy* (St. Louis: C. V. Mosby, 1970), p. 437.
111. *The "brain" is*: Erwin Schrodinger, *What Is Life and Mind and Matter* (Cambridge: Cambridge University Press, 1969), p. 131.
111. "Furthermore, one of": Werner Heisenberg, *Physics and Philosophy* (New York: Harper & Row, 1958), p. 200.
112. *Heisenberg goes on*: Ibid., p. 58.
112. "It has always been": Percy W. Bridgman, *The Nature of Physical Reality* (New York: John Wiley & Sons, 1964), p. 21.
112. "An essential distinction": Ibid., p. 24.
113. *You see it*: Gardner Murphy, "The Boundaries Between the Person and the World," *British Journal of Psychology* 47, no. 2 (May 1956) : 88–94.
113. "As a result": Ludwig von Bertalanffy, *Problems of Life* (New York: John Wiley & Sons, 1952), p. 134.
114. "The time of the mathematician": Bridgman, op. cit., p. 29.
114. "According to modern": Max Planck, cited in LeShan, *The Medium, The Mystic, and The Physicist* (New York: The Viking Press, 1974), pp. 66–67.
115. "Before Clerk Maxwell": Albert Einstein, cited in ibid., p. 67.
115. "The objective world": Herman Weyl, cited in ibid., p. 69.
115. "In man's brief": Linden Barnett, cited in ibid., p. 70.
116. "I turned around": Carlos Castaneda, *Journey to Ixtlan* (New York: Simon & Schuster, 1972), p. 298.
117. *They are born*: J. Krishnamurti, *Freedom from the Known* (New York: Harper & Row, 1969).
117. ". . . our insistent attempt": Bridgman, op. cit., p. 27.
120. "Shibli was asked": Indries Shah, *The Way of the Sufi* (New York: E. P. Dutton & Co., 1970), p. 168.

Chapter 15: REALISTIC ACTION

Page:

135. "Numerous problems today": Donella Meadows et al., *Limits to Growth* (New York: Universe Books, 1972), p. 150.
135. ". . . hardly a task": Willis Harman, Introduction in *Cosmic Consciousness* by Richard M. Bucke (New York: Causeway Books, 1974), p. 5.

135. ". . . trading certain human": Meadows, op. cit., 179–80.
136. "We may be": J. R. Platt, "The Step to Man," *The Futurist,* June 1974
136. "We abuse land": Aldo Leopold, *A Sand County Almanac* (New York: Oxford University Press, 1949), pp. viii–ix.
137. "We are passing": Platt, op. cit.
140. THE THREE PRISONERS: Martin Buber, *Tales of the Hasidim: Later Masters* (New York: Schocken Books, 1948), p. 247.
142. "It is not action": Swami Nikhilananda, trans., *Bhagavad Gita,* p. 106.
143. MUDDY ROAD: Paul Reps, *Zen Flesh, Zen Bones* (Rutland, Vt.: Charles E. Tuttle Co., 1957), p. 18.
147. "Before his death": Martin Buber, *Tales of the Hasidim: Early Masters* (New York: Schocken Books, 1947), p. 251.

Conclusion

Page:

151. THE MAGIC MONASTERY: Idries Shah, *The Magic Monastery* (London: Jonathan Cape, 1972), pp. 13–15.
154. EXCLUSION: Idries Shah, *Thinkers of the East* (London: Jonathan Cape, 1972), p. 33.